Eliza Sawers

Under a Cloud

Eliza Sawers

Under a Cloud

ISBN/EAN: 9783337338985

Printed in Europe, USA, Canada, Australia, Japan

Cover: Foto ©Andreas Hilbeck / pixelio.de

More available books at **www.hansebooks.com**

Under a Cloud

BY

ELIZA SAWERS

Edinburgh

J. MACLAREN, PRINCES STREET

1867

The Memory

OF A BELOVED DAUGHTER,

THIS VOLUME IS INSCRIBED

BY

HER MOTHER.

CONTENTS.

———◦◦◦———

UNDER A CLOUD.

INTRODUCTION.

GO! little book, I send thee forth, God
speed thee on thy way,
Bind up the wounded, bleeding heart, and
Jesus' love display;
Solace the heavy-laden soul, calm thou the troubled
breast,
And may some anxious, seeking souls, in Jesus' arms
find rest.
May little lambs through thee be led, to seek the Lord
in truth,
And He will of them all be found, e'en in their early
youth.
Point out the precious Saviour, to some poor trembling
soul;
Oh! bid the sick to Jesus come, that He may make
them whole.
Go! for the arduous fight of faith, and nerve the
trembling heart,
Them show the crown of amaranth, and strength to
them impart.
Go! cheer the toil-worn pilgrim, and depict his happy
home,

A

Where, all his weary wand'rings o'er, he never more shall
roam.

Go! cheer the lonely mariner, as he speeds o'er the
deep,

Him of that faithful Pilot tell, who doth him safely keep;

Who o'er the stormy main presides, whose proud waves
He can stay,

Who stills the angry billows, and whom raging winds
obey,

Who him will bring through ev'ry storm to Canaan's
tranquil shore,

Where, safely moored, his little bark shall suffer storms
no more.

Go! urge him on who patient runs the swift race set
before him,

Oh! bid him unto Jesus look, whose loving eye is o'er
him;

Him show the glorious triumph palm, the radiant
crown of life,

Awarded by our blessed Lord, to victors in the strife.

Go! dry the mourners' burning tears, them show the
heav'nly land,

Where ev'ry tear is wiped away, by God's own gracious
hand;

Where those loved ones, for whom they mourn, now
lean on Jesus' breast,

And 'neath a Father's loving smile, enjoy *eternal* rest;

Tell them that in a little while, they'll meet on yonder
shore,

Where death and parting are unknown, where joy
reigns evermore.

Go! lead some erring wand'rers home, invite them to
the fold,

To taste a Saviour's deathless love, His mercy to behold ;
Proclaim His invitation kind, "Poor sinner, come to Me,
Thine ev'ry sin I will forgive, life, peace, I'll give to thee."
Go ! tell the guileless little ones, that Jesus will them
    bless,
That if they give themselves to Him, He'll be their
    righteousness ;
That as they tread this desert scene He'll be their
    Guard and Guide,
And their faithful, gentle Shepherd, for ever at their side.
Go ! tell the weary, aged saints, that He will be their
    Stay,
That He will give them grace and strength according
    to their day;
That down the dreary vale of years He'll gently lead
    them on,
That He will keep them day by day, e'en till their
    journey's done.
Go ! and God's blessing go with thee, oh ! may thou
    do some good,
That on that Day it may be said, "She hath done what
    she could."

"THERE SHALL BE NO NIGHT THERE."

NO night of *sorrow* shall be there! all griefs,
    all sighs are o'er,
    No bleeding heart, no tear-dimmed eye, on
      that celestial shore ;
God, with His gentle hand of love, shall wipe all tears
    away,
And in His presence we shall joy, secure in endless
    day.

No night of *sin* can enter there! like Jesus we shall be,
For we shall see Him as He is, and holy be as He;
No wand'ring thoughts, no anxious cares, shall agitate
    our breast,
No sin shall mar our services, in yonder land of rest.

No night of *ignorance* is there ! we 'll know as we are
    known,
And through a blest eternity, rejoice before the throne ;
No clouds shall e'er o'ershadow us,—faith will be
    changed to sight,
All gloomy doubts and fears dispelled, in that sweet land
    of light.

No night of *suffering* is there! no weariness, no pain,
The ransomed in that better land, shall ne'er be sick
    again ;
No aching head, no fevered brow, shall weigh our
    spirit down,
For in Emmanuel's happy land, all sickness is unknown.

No night of *parting* shall be there ! our loved ones gone
    before,
Shall hail us at the gates of bliss, we'll meet to part
    no more,
To be for ever with the Lord, our griefs, our trials o'er,
No tearful eye, no sad farewell, on yonder radiant shore!

No night of *death* shall enter there ! to close our peaceful
    rest,
No tender ties are sever'd, in the mansions of the blest ;
Once in our happy, longed-for home, we'll rest in Jesus'
    love,
For ah ! no night can ever be, in our God's house above.

January 25, 1857.

TO A FRIEND.

 H ! near each other let us live,
 By living near the throne,
Thus, in each other's company,
 We ne'er shall feel alone.

In close communion with our God,
 Let us walk day by day,
And, leaning on His arm of love,
 Pursue our upward way.

May we live in loving converse
 With God, our chiefest Friend,
Assured that to our earnest prayers
 He will an answer send.

ARRAN, *August* 5, 1857.

"*LO! I AM WITH YOU ALWAY.*"

WHEN sundered far, how sweet to meet
Before our Father's mercy-seat !
To pour into His gracious ear
Our ev'ry care, our ev'ry fear.

Ah ! there we would for ever lie,
And realise our Father nigh,
His eye of love He on us bends,
And to our cry, His ear He lends.

We would, O holy Father, rest
Our weary heads upon Thy breast ;
Encircled by Thy loving arm,
We feel secure from ev'ry harm.

Thy gentle hand us all doth guide,
For Thou art ever at our side,
To strengthen, comfort, and to cheer—
For ah ! 'tis Heaven when Thou art near.

ARRAN, *September* 16, 1857.

NEW YEAR'S HYMN.

NOTHER year has passed away, with all
    its griefs and fears,
    But God has cheered our bleeding hearts,
      and wiped away our tears ;
And should our future path be dark, we'll trust our
    Father's power,
Which is most precious to His saints, in sorrow's darkest
    hour.

Another year has passed away—how changed is the
    scene !
Since last we hailed a New Year's Day, how busy
    death has been !
How many friends have safely reached, the bright, the
    better land !
How many homes made desolate, by war's destroying
    hand !

Another year has passed away, with all its toils and
    cares,
But grace has aided us till now, us saved from many
    snares ;
On God we cast our future cares, and on His love
    rely,
He will our ev'ry burden bear, our ev'ry want supply.

Another year has passed away—how great our guilt has
been !
Our words and actions stained with sin, our very
thoughts unclean ;
Oh ! may our souls in Jesus' blood, be this day cleansed
anew,
And, from our heavy load released, the heavenly race
pursue.

Another year has passed away, another stage is o'er
Of our upward, homeward journey, to Canaan's blissful
shore ;
Oh ! let us ever hasten on, prepare to meet our God,
And may daily strength be given us, to tread the thorny
road.

Another year has passed away, our race is nearer run,
Soon will the glorious prize be gained, the crown of
glory won ;
Encouraged by God's cheering voice, we'll press on day
by day,
And, in the prospect bright forget the dangers of the
way.

Another year has passed away, ere long we'll reach our
home,
And receive the gracious welcome, "Ye blessed children,
come,
My precious blood I shed for you, to wash your sins
away,
Come, ever shall you dwell with Me, in realms of
cloudless day."

Another year has passed away—our days are fleeting fast,
We know not but this opening year, may prove to us our
    last,
For ere it shall have run its course, we may have gained
    that shore
Where winds and billows never rise, where tempests
    rage no more.

Another year has passed away—life's day will soon be
    past ;
May this year find us holier and better than the last,
Our hearts more weaned from earthly things, more
    fixed on joys above,
That we our God may glorify and rest in Jesus' love.

Another year has passed away—soon may the summons
    come ;
May our lamps be brightly burning, when Jesus calls us
    home,
To that bright land of light and love, where death can
    enter never,
Where in His presence we shall bask, for ever and for
    ever !

January 1, 1858.

NEW YEAR'S HYMN FOR CHILDREN.

JESUS! bless a pilgrim band,
Travelling to the better land;
Keep us in the narrow way,
Never let us go astray.

Fold us in Thy tender arms,
There we're free from all alarms;
On Thy gentle, loving breast,
Let Thy lambs in safety rest.

May we ever hear Thy voice
Bidding us in Thee rejoice,
Sweetly saying, " Follow Me,
And thy Leader I will be."

All our wants do Thou supply,
Guard our steps with watchful eye,
Guide us by Thy hand of love,
Safely to our home above.

Let the year we now begin,
Find us dying more to sin,
Growing day by day in grace,
Till we see Thee face to face.

May we then rejoicing stand,
With the sheep at Thy right hand,
And, in loudest strains, confess,
" Jesus is our Righteousness."

January 1, 1858.

ALL IS WELL.

 OON life's fondest hopes decay,
    Soon youth's pleasures pass away,
    But, if Jesus be our *Stay*,
        All, all is well.

Oft we are by sins oppress'd,
Oft by doubts and fears distress'd,
But, if Jesus be our *Rest*,
    All, all is well.

Soon earth's brightest joys may end,
And the shades of grief descend,
But, if Jesus be our *Friend*,
    All, all is well.

Dearest friends may leave our side,
Toils and dangers may betide,
But, if Jesus be our *Guide*,
    All, all is well.

Oft our journey seems too long,
Oft afflictions round us throng,
But, if Jesus be our *Song*,
    All, all is well.

Oft we wander in the night,
Oft our joys are lost to sight,
But, if Jesus be our *Light*,
    All, all is well.

Oft our en'mies lie concealed,
And at us their weapons wield,
But, if Jesus be our *Shield*,
    All, all is well.

Oft do cares our peace destroy,
Oft temptations us annoy,
But, if Jesus be our *Joy*,
    All, all is well.

In the dark and cloudy day,
We are very prone to stray,
But, if Jesus be our *Way*,
    All, all is well.

Oft our life is but begun,
When 'tis said, "Thy race is run,"
But, if Jesus be our *Sun*,
    All, all is well.

October 28, 1858.

PRAYER.

 H! let Thy presence go with us,
 Be Thou our constant Friend,
And to our ev'ry prayer and cry,
 Do Thou an answer send.

PROMISE.

Fear thou not, for I am with thee,
 No earthly friend so near,
To hear thy prayer, to mark thy sigh,
 To dry the falling tear.

PRAYER.

Oh! let Thy presence go with us,
 In sorrow's trying day;
Be near to cheer our drooping hearts,
 And wipe the tear away.

PROMISE.

Fear thou not, for I am with thee,
 In sorrow as in joy,
And I will cheer thine aching heart
 When anxious cares annoy.

PRAYER.

Oh ! let Thy presence go with us,
   Watch o'er us day and night,
In times of danger us defend,
   Put all our foes to flight.

PROMISE.

Fear thou not, for I am with thee,
   By night as well as day,
In danger I will thee defend,
   And chase thy fears away.

PRAYER.

Oh ! let Thy presence go with us,
   Be alway at our side,
And in the dark and dreary day,
   For all our wants provide.

PROMISE.

Fear thou not, for I am with thee,
   In sickness as in health,
Upon a bed of languishing,
   In poverty and wealth.

PRAYER.

Oh ! let Thy presence go with us,
   Through all life's little while,
And may we tread this vale of tears
   Cheered onward by Thy smile.

PROMISE.

Fear thou not, for I am with thee,
  I will with thee abide,
And 'neath the covert of My wings,
  Thou mayest ever hide.

PRAYER.

Oh ! let Thy presence go with us,
  When life ebbs fast away,
And when we walk through death's dark vale,
  Be Thou our strength and stay.

PROMISE.

Fear thou not, for I am with thee,
  Until life's latest breath,
I'll clasp thee in Mine arms of love,
  When comes the hour of death.

November 27, 1858.

NEW YEAR'S HYMN.

NOTHER year has joined the past, and
we are nearer home,
Our holy, everlasting home, where death
can never come;
'Tis but a short, a little while we sojourn here below,
Erelong we'll reach Emmanuel's land, nor sin nor
sorrow know.

No pains, no griefs can e'er be felt, on Canaan's tranquil
shore,
For when the morn of joy has dawned, the night of
weeping's o'er;
Then, upward, onward let us haste, pursue life's thorny
way,
Though dark and dreary it may be, it leads to cloudless
day.

The sands of life are falling fast, soon will our race be run,
The battle fought, the conflict o'er, the crown of glory
won—
All our days of mourning ended, with Jesus we shall
reign,
And meet our loved ones gone before, no more to part
again.

Our little bark is gliding on across life's troubled sea,
And though the tempest rage around, we ne'er shall
    moved be—
Each billow shall us only waft, more swiftly to that shore,
Where all is calm, serene, and bright, where ev'ry storm
    is o'er.

How swiftly flows the tide of time ! nor will its moments
    stay,
Then let us love and serve our God, while it is called
    to-day—
The gloomy night wears fast away, another year is past,
And this dreary scene of sorrow, will not for ever last.

For what is life? a passing cloud, a short, a fitful dream,
'Tis a snow-flake on the ocean, a ripple on the stream,
Which for a little while is seen, and then is gone for ever—
Ah ! slender is the thread of life, one moment may it sever.

We will not alway tarry here, this world is not our rest,
Oh ! how consoling is this thought, when weary and
    opprest,
We have a home beyond the skies, a home of peace and
    love,
No sin, no sorrow, pain, nor death, in that bright land
    above !

For all the mercies of the past we this day bless the Lord,
We go forward to the future, depending on His Word—
Oh ! may He be our faithful Friend, in sorrow alway
    near,
To mark our sighs, to hear our prayers, to dry the fall-
    ing tear.

This day life's journey we resume, oh ! may our Father's
    hand,
Still lead and guide us till we reach, the bright, the better
    land,
Where no burning tear of sorrow shall e'er bedim our
    sight,
For all is ceaseless joy and bliss, in yonder realms of light.

There we shall see Him as He is, and know as we are
    known,
And through a blest eternity, we'll bask before the throne;
Clad in Emmanuel's snow-white robe, nought us from
    Him shall sever,
We 'll on His gentle bosom rest, for ever and for ever !

January 1, 1859.

NEW YEAR'S HYMN FOR CHILDREN.

FATHER! bless this glad New Year,
May we spend it in Thy fear,
As in years, in wisdom grow,
More and more of Jesus know.

Cleanse us all anew from sin,
Let Thy Spirit dwell within,
Mould us to Thy will divine
Till we in Thy likeness shine.

Grant us grace from day to day,
To pursue the heav'nly way—
Rough and thorny though it be,
It will lead us home to Thee.

When we're weary and opprest,
Bid us come to Thee for rest—
Gently whisper, "Trust in Me,
And thy refuge I will be."

Let Thy love our footsteps guide,
Keep us alway at Thy side,
Lead us by Thy gracious hand,
To the bright, the better land.

There we'll see Thee as Thou art,
There we'll meet no more to part,
And with all the ransomed throng,
Jesus! *Thou* shalt be our Song!

January 1, 1859.

"*IT IS I.*"

IN sorrow's dark and dreary hour,
　　Be Thou, O Jesus, nigh,
To dry the eye bedimmed with tears,
　　To whisper, "It is I."

When all life's cherished hopes are fled,
　　When loved ones fade and die,
Be near to soothe our bleeding heart,
　　To whisper, "It is I."

When laid upon a bed of pain,
　　Oh ! listen to our cry,
Bid all our anxious fears depart,
　　And whisper, "It is I."

When all around is gloomy night,
　　When clouds obscure our sky,
Oh ! may we hear Thy gentle voice,
　　Fond whisp'ring, "It is I."

Then, though the winds and billows rage,
　　We will the storm defy,
For still we'll hear Thy voice of love,
　　Soft whisp'ring, "It is I."

When those we love do faithless prove,
  Do Thou their place supply ;
Oh ! bid us trust *Thy* deathless love,
  And whisper, " It is I."

When passing through the vale of death,
  We 'll on Thy love rely,
Thou wilt sustain our trembling heart,
  Wilt whisper, " It is I."

And when we see Thee face to face,
  In our loved home on high,
Then shall we praise our Saviour-God,
  Who whispered, " It is I."

January 25, 1859.

"*COME UNTO ME.*"

"COME unto Me," O *tempted* one,
    And lean upon My breast,
For I have felt temptation's power,
    And I can give thee rest.

"Come unto Me," O *doubting* one,
    By guilt and sins distrest,
Have I not suffered all for thee ?
    Then I will give thee rest.

"Come unto Me," O *seeking* one,
    When weary and opprest,
Thy portion I will ever be,
    And I will give thee rest.

"Come unto Me," O *mourning* one,
    When by afflictions prest,
Repose on Me thine aching head,
    And I will give thee rest.

"Come unto Me," O *dying* one,
    Thy soul, with peace possest,
Shall calmly tread the vale of death,
    Then enter into rest.

" Come unto Me," O *ransomed* one,
Now art thou fully blest,
Here shalt thou dwell in endless peace,
And with *Me* ever rest.

January, 30, 1859,

THE SABBATH.

HAIL, hallowed day!
 Things of earth pass away.
Our souls be raised to joys above,
That we may seek our Father's face,
May praise the riches of His grace,
 Adore His deathless love,
  On His own day!

  Sweet day of rest!
 Welcome to souls opprest,
Its sacred hours be spent with God,
In holy thoughts be passed the day,
Of Him who is " the Life, the Way,"
 Who, by His precious blood,
  Hath made us blest!

  To praise and pray,
 On God's own holy day,
Up to His house with joy we 'll go,
To hear of Jesus' love divine,
That we may in His image shine,
 May more Him love and know,
  From day to day!

But if alone,
We 'll bend before the throne,
And with the saints we 'll praise the Lord.
Then may we feel His presence nigh,
Then may He listen to our cry,
And to us, in His Word,
Himself make known!

This day God blest;
May peace pervade our breast,
To us, oh! may it ever prove,
The foretaste of that sinless morrow,
On which shall fall no night of sorrow;
For in God's house above,
All, all is rest!

Hail, glorious day!
Whose first calm dawning ray
Saw Jesus from the grave arise,
Victor o'er death and all our foes;
We now in Him have sweet repose,
And with Him in the skies,
We 'll reign for aye!

February 15, 1859.

THE HAPPY HOME.

THERE is a home, 'tis better far,
   Than any earthly home can be,
'Tis brighter than the brightest star,
   'Tis lasting as eternity !

No sin doth break its calm rest ever,
   No grief doth cloud its happy day,
The tide of joy flows on for ever,
   For God hath wiped all tears away !

No darkness there ! no dreary night
   Doth on that bright home ever fall,
The Lamb's its pure, its perfect light,
   Its life, its joy, its all in all !

And in that holy, happy home,
   Loved friends do meet no more to sever,
For *there* no changes e'er can come,
   There all is love and bliss for ever !

Oh ! happy land of spirits bright,
   May we all hail thy portals fair,
Enter at death thy realms of light,
   And rest and reign with Jesus there !

March 19, 1859.

TO ELIZABETH.

 NOTHER year has passed away
Since last I hailed thy natal day:
How many changes hast thou seen!
For ah, how busy death has been!

How few and fleeting are thy days!
Then spend them to thy Saviour's praise,
For soon the night of death may come,
And call thee to thy happy home.

A pilgrim in a stranger-land,
May Jesus guide thee by His hand,
Until, thy weary wanderings o'er,
Thou safe arrive on Canaan's shore.

Should dark afflictions round thee rise,
Should bitter tears bedim thine eyes,
Oh! stay on God thy mourning soul,
He will the waves of grief control.

Trust in the Lord, He cares for thee,
Thy Father and thy God He'll be;
In light or shade, still trust His love,
And fix thy heart and hopes above.

When weary, lonely, and opprest,
Lean on thy Saviour's loving breast,
Oh! cast on Him thine anxious cares,
He all thy griefs and trials shares.

When cherished friends around thee die,
When loved ones wing their flight on high,
Oh ! are they not for ever blest ?
And do they not in Jesus rest ?

Ah, yes ! their every conflict's o'er,
Sin and temptation grieve no more,
They dwell with Christ in endless day,
Their tears for ever wiped away.

And when thy work on earth is done,
And when the sands of life are run,
Jesus will take thee to His home,
Where from Himself thou ne'er shalt roam.

Fear not to stem the swelling tide,
For Jesus will be at thy side,
Around thee will His arms be cast,
Till Jordan's gloomy waves be past.

Then onward, onward, home to God,
Nor fear life's darksome, dang'rous road,
Thy God will lead thee safely on,
Till all thy pilgrim days be done.

For He on whom thy hopes depend,
He is thy Guardian and thy Friend,
Then, on His grace and love rely,
Until thou reach thy home on high.

April 26, 1859.

JESUS OUR ALL.

OFT we are by sins opprest,
Oft by doubts and fears distrest,
But our terrors all shall cease
If Thou, Jesus, be our *Peace*.

Oft we wander in the night,
Oft our joys are lost to sight,
But we ne'er shall go astray,
If Thou, Jesus, be our *Way*.

Oft do waves of sorrow roll,
And well-nigh o'erwhelm our soul,
But we will not fear the shock,
If thou, Jesus, be our *Rock*.

Oft do foes around us throng,
Oft the conflict's fierce and long,
But our en 'mies all must yield,
If Thou, Jesus, be our *Shield*.

Oft our journey seems too long,
Oft our foes are fierce and strong,
But we'll reach our home at length,
If thou, Jesus, be our *Strength*.

Soon will end life's little day,
Soon we all shall pass away,
But our path will not seem long,
If thou, Jesus, be our *Song*.

April 28, 1859.

SPRING.

HAIL, gentle Spring ! thou welcome art,
  To Nature and to me ;
  Bright hope revives within this heart
  When I thy flow'rets see.

They tell me dreary winter's o'er,
  Its storms all past and gone,
They, with their varied, lovely tints,
  Rejoice 'neath yonder sun.

The valleys clad in glowing green,
  Refresh the weary eye,
The balmy gales, the blossoms fair,
  Proclaim glad summer nigh.

All Nature smiles ! all, all is bright,
  The woods with joy do ring,
The heart of man is also glad,
  For beauteous is the Spring !

April 30, 1859.

SUMMER.

BRIGHT summer's come! sweet summer's
    here!
  With all its flow'rets gay,
The feathered songsters of the grove,
  Carol the livelong day.

Again the lily decks the vale,
  The woodbine and the rose,
The bright blue sweet forget-me-not,
  Its tiny leaves unclose.

How varied Nature's beauties are
  In this fair summer-time!
The waving fields, the verdant vales,
  The hills we love to climb.

'Tis sweet to wander forth at eve,
  And hear the blackbird's song,
Oh! may we join him in the praise,
  Which doth to God belong!

May, 21, 1859.

AUTUMN.

HOW thickly fall the withered leaves !
    Proclaiming man must die ;
May we prepare in summer-time,
    For our bright home on high.

They point us to that dreary day,
    When death shall lay us low,
When as a dream we 'll pass away,
    From all things here below.

But trees again shall bud and bloom,
    When winter's storms are o'er,
And we, too, from the grave shall rise,
    To flourish evermore !

Ah, yes ! we 'll bloom in paradise,
    Close by the Tree of Life ;
There all is joyous, endless spring !
There all 's with beauty rife !

June 25, 1859.

WINTER.

STERN winter comes with chill cold winds,
 And lays all Nature low ;
The tempest howls o'er hills and dale,
 The streamlets cease to flow.

Yet winter hath its pleasures too,
 For round the blazing hearth
The gladsome tale, the merry song,
 Fill hearts with joy and mirth.

All Nature's dead ! no flow'rets bloom,
 For 'tis a lovely sight
To see the trees, the fields, the hills,
 All clad in robes of white.

How pure is the untrodden snow !
 Can ought with it e'er vie ?
Ah, yes ! souls washed in Jesus' blood,
 Meet for their home on high !

June 30, 1859.

THE BETTER LAND.

HERE is a *land*—a sinless land,
 Where sorrow ne'er shall be,
No sin can e'er invade that land,
 May we its glories see.

There is a *shore*—a peaceful shore,
 Where storms for ever cease;
Where winds and waves distress no more,
 Where all is calm and peace.

There is a *home*—a heavenly home,
 From sin and suff'ring free,
There friends shall meet to part no more,
 And ever blessed be.

There is a *band*—a joyful band,
 Around the throne on high;
For God hath wiped away all tears
 From ev'ry weeping eye.

There is a *throne*—a radiant throne,
 Before which we shall stand,
And sing the new, th' eternal song,
 In that bright, better land.

There is a *crown*—a crown of life,
   Which fadeth not away;
Reserved for they who love the Lord,
   And they shall reign for aye.

There is a *Tree*—the Tree of Life,
   That blossoms near the throne;
And they who taste its precious fruit,
   Shall know as they are known.

There is a *book*—the Book of Life,
   Oh! may our names be there;
May we be of the faithful few
   Who Heaven's bliss shall share.

There is a *Lamb*—a spotless Lamb,
   Before the throne of God;
Oh wondrous love! amazing grace,
   For us He shed His blood.

There is a *stream*—a narrow stream
   Between us and that home,
But Jesus will us safely guide
   When to its brink we come.

These are the hopes that cheer our souls
   Whilst in this vale of tears,
They point us to a fairer scene,
   And chase away our fears.

Then let us, with a lively faith,
Pursue our pilgrim way,
Assured that in that better land
We all shall rest for aye !

July 5, 1859.

MIDNIGHT PRAYER.

IN the lone midnight hour, when all Nature's at
  rest,
  When balmy sleep leaves us we 'll lean on Thy
   breast,
Breathe into Thine ear all our griefs and our fears,
And moisten our couch with true penitent tears.

'Tis sweet, oh ! how sweet, though we bend not the
  knee,
In the still silent night to hold converse with Thee,
Unseen and unknown unto Thee we draw nigh,
Who look 'st on the heart, who will mark ev 'ry sigh.

Oh ! then may we seize that calm, hallowed hour,
Our wants to make known, all our griefs to out-pour,
When sad and opprest Thou, our God, wilt us cheer,
Thine own gracious hand will dry each falling tear.

We will pillow our head on Thy bosom of love,
Thine arm thrown around us, our Friend Thou wilt
  prove,
The day-dawn will find us alone still with Thee,
In near, close communion our souls lost will be.

July 10, 1859.

IN MEMORY OF A BELOVED MOTHER.

N this deeply sad day to Jesus I'll flee,
My Strength and my Stay, my Refuge He'll be;
When I'm sad and opprest on Him I will lean,
Who has my best Portion, my Comforter, been.

I have trod many steps of my pilgrim way,
Since thou didst, my Mother, from earth pass away;
To thee sudden death was sudden glory,
For, in a moment, was finished life's story.

No bitter farewell thy tender heart wrung,
No parting tear-drop from thy meek eye sprung;
Thy Saviour was with thee in death's dreary vale,
His arms of love round thee, thy heart would not fail.

Then landed in safety on that calm, tranquil shore,
Thy sorrows were ended, life's battle was o'er;
Hailed by thy loved ones, so dear to thy heart,
Thou didst meet them all there ne'er from them to part.

And we, too, shall join thee in that peaceful home,
Where no parting, no pain, no sin can e'er come;
Then let me thee follow to that bright land of bliss,
For who would live alway in a cold world like this.

Ah! welcome then, sorrow, and welcome then, pain,
If only with Jesus in bliss I shall reign;
Thrice happy the day when from earth I shall go,
And join my fond loved ones no change e'er to know.

———oo⁞◦⁞oo———

*ANSWER TO THE FOREGOING LINES FROM THE
LOVED ONE IN GLORY.*

H! weep not for me, for I now am at rest,
I safely have reached the bright home of
the blest;
My sufferings are o'er and my tears wiped
away,
And I ever shall bask in glory's bright day.

Then haste thee on, fear not, and thou too shalt rest
Thy now bleeding heart on thy Saviour's fond breast;
His arms of love round us, nought e'er shall us sever,
We'll rest in His love for ever and ever.

We'll follow the Lamb whereso'er He may lead,
By the still waters, or by yon verdant mead;
Then weep not, oh! weep not, but look thou on high,
And see me rejoicing 'neath His loving eye.

Then onward, still onward, though lone be thy way,
Home it will lead thee to the bright realms of day;
Where I now am resting beneath Jesus' smile,
The trials all ended of life's little while.

And when thy work is done again shall we meet,
Thy loved ones in glory with joy shall thee greet ;
And through cloudless day with Jesus we 'll reign,
Nor sorrow, nor sin, nor e 'er suffer again !

ARRAN, *August* 5, 1859.

ACROSTIC.

 LL, all was hushed at evening's close,
R omantic isle! when first thy hills
R ose glorious to my raptured sight,
A ll Nature seemed so calm, so bright,
N ought marred its deep repose.

ARRAN, *August* 8, 1859.

SUNSHINE.

ALL Nature rejoices
   'Neath a bright cloudless sky,
Then let man, too, be glad
   In his Saviour on high ;
Bright Sun of Righteousness,
   'Neath whose calm cheering ray,
We may alway rejoice,
   E'en in life's gloomiest day.

May we now be happy,
   By Jesus' love blest ;
Then in sunshine or shade,
   In Him we shall rest ;
In Nature around us,
   His hand we shall see ;
Walk with Him, love Him,
   And serve Him shall we.

Through hill and through valley,
   Through mountain and stream,
Yea, through all God's works
   His glory doth gleam ;

Then with grateful hearts, may we
His goodness adore,
And learn from all Nature
Him to praise more and more.

ARRAN, *August* 10, 1859.

SHADE.

HEN dark clouds are lowering,
   When no sun appears ,
When Nature is weeping,
   And we full of tears ;
Behind the clouds, sweet then,
   With faith's eye to see,
The sun shining brightly,
   Then cheerful we 'll be.

For Jesus, our Better Sun,
   Shines ever on high,
And we 'll bask in His light,
   Though clouds dim our sky ;
By faith we shall see Him,
   And feel Him most near,
When dark clouds are darkest,
   When Nature 's most drear.

Nought e'er can us sever
   From His fond loving heart,
Not sorrow, not suffering,
   Not death can us part ;

c

Then we 'll cleave to Him close,
Though gloomy our way,
For ere long it will end
In bright, cloudless day.

ARRAN, *August* 11, 1859.

TO THE RAINBOW.

AIL, covenant bow ! in mercy given,
To lead the soul from earth to heaven,
Sweet pledge of peace from God to man,
Thou, with thine arch, the heaven dost span.

'Tis sweet, when days are dark and drear,
To see thee in the cloud appear ;
We know that all beyond is bright,
Though to the eye 'tis dark as night.

Bright emblem, thou, of love divine !
As ages roll thou 'lt radiant shine
Around God's throne of glory bright,
Like to an emerald in sight.

For in that land of perfect light
There are no clouds, no gloomy night,
Our Better Sun doth shine for ever,
There darkness, storms, can enter never !

ARRAN, *August* 30, 1859.

ACROSTIC

 LOVE to wander 'mid thy hills,
S o lofty and so bright;
L ight beams within thy cottage-homes,
E 'en in the darkest night.

O ! how I love thy peaceful vales,
F or fresh and balmy are thy gales.

A h ! thou art ever dear to me,
R omantic island of the sea,
R ichest verdure clothes thy fields,
A nd the gay flower sweet fragrance yields.
N owhere more beauty can there be.

ARRAN, *Sept.* 1, 1859.

THE STREAM.

S the streamlet floweth onward
   Into its parent sea,
So, Holy Father, would our souls
   Seek their calm rest in Thee.

Ever *onwards* doth it flow,
   Thrice happy in its race,
So may we hasten homewards,
   Till lost in Thine embrace.

Oft-times gliding, oft-times dashing,
   Still onward it will run,
Nought shall e'er its course impede
   Until its journey's done.

So may we never tarry,
   But keep the heav'nly road,
Until we lose ourselves in Thee,
   Our Father, and our God!

ARRAN, *Sept.* 4, 1859.

"*JESUS WEPT.*"

"JESUS wept;" sweet precious words
To ev'ry mourning heart,
They cheer the lonely friendless one,
They deepest peace impart.

"Jesus wept;" the mighty God
Shed tears of bitter grief,
And He is near whene'er we call
To give us sweet relief.

"Jesus wept;" O wondrous love!
To Him was sorrow known,
And now He shares our griefs and fears,
We bear them not alone.

"Jesus wept;" the Man of Sorrows,
Upon the throne above,
Still feels with us in all our griefs—
His heart, His name is Love!

"Jesus wept;" He weeps with us,
For He is still the same
As when He wept o'er Lazarus dead,
"Unchanging" is His name.

" Jesus wept ;" the Son of Man,
　And yet the mighty God,
Is still the same fond loving Friend
　As when the earth He trod.

" Jesus wept ;" then when a friend
　Is snatched from our embrace,
We 'll cling to Him in that dark hour,
　And meekly seek His face.

" Jesus wept ;" the Rock of Ages,
　Whose mercy faileth never !
He 's the same to-day, yesterday,
　For ever, and for ever !

" Jesus wept ;" that Friend of friends,
　On whose love we may rest,
The pillow of the weary soul,
　The stay of the opprest.

" Jesus wept ;" then let us go
　To Him in ev'ry sorrow,
He will us cheer, and point our souls
　To Heaven's bright to-morrow.

ARRAN, *Sept.* 10, 1859.

TO THE ROBIN RED-BREAST.

 LOVE to hear thy merry chirp
  At early dawn of day,
I love, when all around is calm,
  To hear thy matin lay.

Thou teachest man to praise his God
  Ere yet his toils begin,
To ask of Him throughout the day
  To keep him from all sin.

I love to see thee at the door,
  Or on the window-sill,
Picking up the smallest crumbs,
  There welcome thee I will.

And then in winter's stormy days,
  When all is dark and drear,
Thou com'st into my cottage home,
  The lonely heart to cheer.

And, then again, at eventide,
  When all is still and bright,
I love to hear thy song of praise,
  Ere fall the shades of night.

Só may I then, too, bless the Lord,
　For all His mercies kind,
And, ere I give myself to sleep,
　His goodness call to mind.

For ah ! if God doth care for thee,
　Ne'er shall His children want,
He will their heart's desires fulfil,
　Their ev'ry prayer will grant.

Then may I, little bird, like thee,
　Upon His care rely,
For to the waiting, longing soul
　Our God is ever nigh !

ARRAN, *Sept.* 12, 1859.

NIGHT.

IGHT is the time to *rest*,
To lay us down to sleep,
Trusting in God, our faithful Guard,
Who will us safely keep.

Night is the time to *pray*,
To raise the thoughts on high,
To hold communion with our God
When He alone is nigh.

Night is the time to *weep*,
To mourn o'er ev'ry sin,
Humbly to ask our gracious God
To whisper peace within.

Night is the time to *think*,
To commune with our heart,
To meditate on love divine,
And choose the better part.

Night is the time to *watch*,
To fear the tempter's power,
But Jesus will be near to aid
In that dark, trying hour.

Night is the time to *praise*,
To bless God for His love,
To waft our souls from earth to heaven,
And join the choir above.

Night is the time to *joy*,
To bask 'neath Jesus' smiles,
Rejoicing in His boundless love
Who weariness beguiles.

Night is the time to *die*,
To shed the latest tear,
To lay us in the arms of love,
And soar to yon bright sphere.

ARRAN, *September 20, 1859.*

ACROSTIC.

ISLE of beauty, fair are thy vales !
S o soft and balmy are thy gales ,
L ovely are thy heath-clad hills,
E ver rippling are thy rills.

O h, earth has not a lovelier spot !
F or thou, once seen, art ne'er forgot.

A ll Nature smiles beneath thy sky ;
R omantic isle ! *all* charms the eye !
R obed in such grace and beauty rare,
A nd decked with flow'rets bright and fair,
N o spot can e'er with thee compare !

ARRAN, *September* 24, 1859.

MOONLIGHT.

ONE night, when all was hushed and still,
As slow I wandered up the hill,
The silver moon, with placid ray,
Rose calmly o'er fair Brodick Bay.

The scene was peace ! all Nature slept,
While lofty Goatfell his watch kept
O'er sweet Glen Rosa's tranquil vale,
O'er stream and glen, o'er hill and dale.

Methought how peaceful is this scene !
As if no curse had ever been ;
All Nature lay in deep repose,
No dark clouds dimm'd that evening's close.

How bright thou shinest, queen of night !
How sweet to roam 'neath thy calm light,
When all around is fair and still,
And nought heard save the murmuring rill !

'Tis then I love to walk alone,
And muse on former joys now gone,
When loving friends around me moved ;
But, ah ! how many faithless proved.

Yet there were some more fond, more true,
When days were dark, and friends were few,
Who gently lent their aid to cheer
And comfort me when all was drear.

And there is One who ne'er will leave,
Who 'll closer than a brother cleave ;
For, ah ! when life is dark and drear,
That loving Friend is alway near.

Then, oh ! how sweet, when stars are bright,
To wander forth by calm moonlight,
Alone with God, to feel Him near,
To breathe our griefs into His ear.

But change the scene ; perchance some friend,
On whom our fondest hopes depend,
May walk with us at that still hour,
And vows exchange, and thoughts outpour.

Then, gentle moon, we love thy light,
Dark but for thee would be the night,
Cheerless without thy silver ray,
Which changes night to lightsome day.

Then, welcome, welcome, lovely queen !
Thou sheddest beauty o'er this scene ;
Remembered long will be this night,
Its memories treasured with delight.

And should I ne'er revisit more,
O lovely isle ! thy tranquil shore,
By me can ne'er forgotten be,
The happy days I spent in thee.

ARRAN, *September* 29, 1859.

"*THIS DO IN REMEMBRANCE OF ME.*"

ORD JESUS ! on this Sabbath-day
 Draw very nigh to me,
And, seated at Thy holy table,
 I will remember Thee.

Remember all Thy sufferings,
 Which Thou didst bear for me,
Thy bitter tears, Thy sore distress—
 Yes, I'll remember Thee.

Remember dark Gethsemane,
 Its fearful agony,
When all Thy friends Thee left and fled—
 Yes, I'll remember Thee.

Remember all Thy dreary path,
 Thy death on Calvary,
For Thou didst die that I might live—
 Yes, I'll remember Thee.

Remember all Thy pains and groans
 When on the bitter tree,
The hidings of Thy Father's face—
 Yes, I'll remember Thee.

Remember sweet Mount Olivet,
　Thee there in prayer I see,
Mount Tabor, too, and Bethany—-
　Yes, I 'll remember Thee.

May I enjoy communion near,
　And very happy be,
Oh, may I taste Thy precious love
　As I rememember Thee !

When from the Mount I shall descend,
　Be near, be near to me,
That I may closely walk with Thee,
　And aye remember Thee.

Thy sweet command, " Remember Me,"
　Shall ne'er forgotten be,
For till this pulse has ceased to beat,
　I will remember Thee.

When earthly tables are withdrawn,
　Then face to face I 'll see,
And through eternity's bright day
　I will remember Thee.

"*LORD, REMEMBER ME.*"

LORD! on this holy festal day,
   Oh! draw me near to Thee,
   Cause shine on me Thy loving face,
   Jesus! remember me.

And as anew I dedicate
   My heart and soul to Thee,
Accept my vows, and hear my prayers,
   Jesus! remember me.

Oh! whilst I tread this vale of tears,
   May I repose on Thee,
In sorrow's dark and cloudy day,
   Jesus! remember me.

When burdened with a sense of sin,
   To Thy breast I will flee,
Speak pardon to my troubled soul,
   Jesus! remember me.

When laid upon a bed of pain,
   I'll raise my soul to Thee;
Oh! give me grace to bear Thy will,
   Jesus! remember me.

And if reviled for Thy dear name,
   I 'll suffer all for Thee,
Meekly I 'll bear reproach and shame,
   Jesus ! remember me.

And should my path be calm and bright,
   May I remember Thee,
When sunshine gilds my onward way,
   Jesus ! remember me.

When comes the solemn hour of death,
   That calls me home to Thee,
Be with me in the dreary vale,
   Jesus ! remember me.

Then welcome me to Heaven's joys,
   Where I 'll Thy glory see,
And, seated on Thy radiant throne,
   Jesus ! remember me.

Then shall I commune face to face
   My Saviour-God, with Thee,
And, through a blest eternity,
   Jesus ! remember me.

October 30, 1859.

TO JEANIE.

THE Lord thee bless,
    Give thee deep peace,
    On this auspicious day ;
    To thee draw near,
  Thy prayers to hear,
For grace to keep His way.

Oh ! rest awhile,
'Neath Jesus' smile,
Ere thou pursue thy way ,
  Review the past,
  Cares on Him cast,
Make Him thy Strength and Stay.

Work, watch, and pray,
  While it is day,
For soon the night will come ;
  Up, be doing,
  Still pursuing,
Till Jesus call thee home.

On His fond breast
For ever rest,
In sorrow's cloudy day;
He will be near
To soothe and cheer,
And wipe.the tear away.

Should storms arise,
Oh! lift thine eyes
To Him whom winds obey;
Lean on His arm,
Secure from harm,
In life's beclouded day.

Walk with thy God,
Keep thou His Word,
And daily grow in grace;
Oh! love Him more,
His name adore,
Until thou see His face.

Praise thou the Lord,
Who shed His blood
From death to ransom thee;
Then to Him cleave,
He'll ne'er deceive,
But will thy Portion be.

Oh! do not fear
When danger's near,
But 'neath His wing abide;
Then trust in Him,
Keep close to Him,
He's alway at thy side.

Life's but a day
Which fleets away,
A short, a transient dream;
Years swiftly glide,
None here abide,
All hasten down the stream.

Then onward haste,
Time do not waste,
Its precious hours redeem;
Thy home of love,
In realms above,
With glory bright doth gleam.

Dear friend, adieu,
Thy path pursue
To realms of cloudless light,
Where thou shalt rest,
Redeemed and blest,
Arrayed in robes of white.

Oh! there may we
Together be,
For ever and for ever;
Where all is joy,
Without alloy,
For sin there enters never!

November 8, 1859.

THE STORM AT SEA.

MARK IV. 35 TO END.

'TWAS eve, the sun had glorious set
  Behind yon lofty hill,
Calm was the Sea of Galilee,
  All was serene and still,

When to the shore of that calm lake
  Came Jesus with His band,
That band of faithful followers,
  Who were at His command.

A bark lay there, they entered in,
  "Launch forth," the Saviour said,
" And let us cross to yonder side,"
  That moment they obeyed.

Now gently did that little bark
  Float o'er that tranquil lake,
Till, suddenly, a storm arose,
  Then they for fear did quake.

Dark was the night, the wind did howl,
  Loud roared the angry sea,
That little crew, o'erwhelmed with dread,
  Ah ! whither did they flee ?

But where was *now* the wearied Lord ?
  Asleep on yonder pillow,
The storm disturbed not *His* repose,
  Nor yet the raging billow.

And why ? because He gently slept
  Upon His Father's breast,
Ah ! there no tempests e'er could beat
  To mar His tranquil rest.

To Him they fled in that dark hour,
  And woke Him out of sleep—
" Master," they cried, " save ! else we sink
  Down in this yawning deep."

Calmly He rose, rebuked the storm,
  Said gently, " Peace, be still,"
Then all was calm, the wind and waves
  Obeyed His mighty will.

And, turning to the trembling twelve,
  " Where is your faith ?" said He,
" Oh ! why so fearful ? trust in Me,
  I will your Refuge be."

" The Pilot's part I will perform,
  No ill shall you betide,
This little bark I 'll guide and guard
  Till safe on yonder side."

And it was so; those chosen ones,
　Led by so sure a Guide,
Did reach ere long the other shore,
　Crossed safe to "yonder side."

Thus floats the Christian's little bark
　O'er life's tempestuous main,
And, spite of winds and angry waves,
　The port of peace 'twill gain.

The winds may roar, the billows rage,
　Dark clouds may dim the sky,
But 'midst the storm we'll hear a voice
　Soft whisp'ring, "It is I."

How oft that whisper calms our fears
　When all around is night!
How precious is that voice of love!
　Transforming all to light.

It bids the stormy waves be still,
　And all is calm and peace,
It soothes our weary, anguished souls,
　And all our sorrows cease.

Jesus! do Thou us safely keep,
　Be Thou our Guard and Guide,
Until our little bark lies moored
　All safe on "yonder side."

And when we reach the port of peace,
　The storms of life all o'er,
We'll bless the hand that led us safe
　To yonder peaceful shore.

December 1, 1859.

NEW YEAR'S HYMN.

"TIME is short," Christian,
  Years pass swift o'er thee,
Night's fleeting, Christian,
  Day is before thee.
Bright will the morrow prove,
  Lasting for ever!
In thy loved home above
  Night shall be never!

Press forward, Christian,
  Home is before thee;
Faint thou not, Christian,
  God's eye is o'er thee.
From His deep heart of love
  Nought shall thee sever!
He will thy Portion prove,
  Now, and for ever!

O'er life's sea, Christian,
  Jesus will guide thee;
Brave the storm, Christian,
  His love will hide thee.
Soon wilt thou gain the shore,
  There rest for ever!
There billows rage no more,
  Storms assail never!

Face the foe, Christian,
　　Love's banner's o'er thee,
Fight the fight, Christian,
　　Glory's before thee.
Bear the cross, banish fear,
　　Be dismayed never;
Through all life's changing year,
　　Trust in God ever!

Onward haste! Christian,
　　"Faint, yet pursuing."
Time redeem, Christian,
　　Be up and doing.
Soon will the race be run,
　　Then joy for ever!
Soon will the crown be won,
　　Which fadeth never!

The Bridegroom comes! Christian,
　　Be thy lamp burning,
Watch and wait, Christian,
　　For His returning.
Morning dawns, glory's near,
　　Slumber then never!
Soon will thy Lord appear,
　　Then bliss for ever!

January 1, 1860.

NEW YEAR'S HYMN FOR CHILDREN.

" The Lord is my Shepherd."—*Psal.* xxiii. 1.

 JESUS ! Shepherd of the sheep,
To Thee the lambs are dear,
Then let Thy love me safely keep
Throughout life's changing year.

May I Thy gentle voice obey,
And closely follow Thee,
For I am very prone to stray,
Then, Jesus, lead Thou me.

Oh ! fold me to Thy loving breast,
And keep me safe from harm,
There may Thy lamb securely rest
Encircled by Thine arm.

For all my wants do Thou provide,
Watch o'er me day by day,
Be Thou my Guardian and my Guide
Through all my homeward way.

Lord, in the year I now begin,
May I more holy be,
And may I daily die to sin
Till meet to dwell with Thee.

Then may I in the fold above
Among Thy flock appear,
And praise Thee, Jesus, for Thy love
Through Heaven's eternal year !

January 1, 1860.

THE SEA.

I LOVE to wander by the shore
  At morning, noon, or night,
To gaze upon the deep blue sea
  Inspires me with delight,
To watch its constant ebb and flow
  When all is fair and bright.

What are the thoughts that fill the mind
  Whilst gazing on the sea ?
Does it not speak of love divine,
  Of Jesus' love to me ?.
Does it not also image forth
  A bright eternity?

When raging storms its bosom swells,
  When waves are mountains high,
When winds are howling down the glens,
  And gloomy is the sky,
I love to seat me on the shore
  And gaze on *silently.*

'Tis thus, methinks, the soul is tost,
  When doubts and fears rush in,
Whene'er the wily tempter's near
  Unveiling ev'ry sin.
'Tis then the bosom heaves with fear,
  And all is gloom within.

But Jesus comes ! says, " Peace, be still,
  Did I not die for thee ?"
Then Satan flees, and all is rest,
  Clouds, fears, and doubts *all* flee ;
A deep calm peace pervades the soul
  Like to that tranquil sea.

When not a ripple stirs its breast
  To mark its ebb or flow,
When not a cloud obscures the sky,
  When not a breeze doth blow,
When all is hushed, and calm, and bright,
  Above, around, below,

Then oh ! how sweet to wander forth
  And list the billows' roar !
And as I gaze across the sea,
  To think of " yonder shore,"
Where winds shall rise and billows swell,
  Where tempests rage no more !

January 5, 1860.

TO DEAR LIZZIE.

 NOTHER year has passed away,
And this is now thy natal day;
Then listen, Lizzie dear, to me,
Whilst I a loving word give thee.

Thou hast now fourteen summers seen,
God through them has thy Father been;
From dangers He has kept thee free,
A Guard, a Guide, He's been to thee.

Oh! list His words, " Give Me thine heart,"
Choose thou, my child, the better part,
Which no one e'er can take away.
Oh! tread, e'en now, the narrow way.

It leads to life, to joys above;
Then come to Jesus! taste His love;
He loves the little lambs to bless,
He will be all thy Righteousness.

Then give to Him thy life's fresh morn;
He will with grace thy soul adorn,
Will be through life thy constant Friend,
Will guide thee to thy journey's end.

Temptations may thy peace destroy,
Sins, sorrows, cares may thee annoy,
But if in Jesus, all is well,
He will thy doubts and fears dispel.

May many sunny years be thine,
May God's love on thy pathway shine,
Until, thy pilgrim days all o'er,
Thou plant thy foot on Canaan's shore.

That I may meet thee, loved one, there,
Is thy fond Mother's earnest prayer ;
For ah ! in yonder world of joy
No sorrows e'er shall us annoy.

And now, adieu, I thee commend
To God, thine ever faithful Friend ;
Accept thy Mother's loving lay,
On this thy happy natal day.

January 13, 1860.

ON FRIENDSHIP.

HOW precious is a friend
On whom we may depend ;
 Whose love
Can chase our tears away ;
Can turn to day
The darkest night of grief ;
Can bring us sweet relief,
And soothe us midst our woe :
Our tears then cease to flow ;
 Their voice
Bids us rejoice.

Their sympathy is sweet,
When at the mercy-seat,
 We meet
In lowly earnest prayer.
God hears us there !
He listens to our cry,
Us blesses from on high.
When all around is night
Their presence brings us light :
 Tears cease,
And all is peace.

But should that friend prove cold,
Should we no love behold,
    We weep,
And turn from them away
To Him, who aye
Doth love His children dear ;
Who doth the lonely cheer ;
Who points us to that Friend
Whose love can know no end ;
    Whose smile
Doth grief beguile.

Oft friendship's but a name ;
How oft we prove the same
    Whilst here !
The truest friends deceive ;
The fondest leave,
And we are left alone.
Yet ah ! is there not One
Who 'll to us closely cleave,
Who ne 'er will us deceive ?
    He 's near,
When all is drear.

January 19, 1860.

ON LOVE.

Y daughter said, "O! write on Love."
To please her I will try.
Love's not confined to Heaven above;
The human heart doth oft it prove;
Then will I now comply.

Love visits earth, and Love is sweet,
A balm to mortals given,
For ah ! 'tis precious when we meet
A kindred heart, 'tis then we greet
A boon sent us from Heaven.

Love dwells in ev'ry social breast;
For cold that heart must be
Which cannot feel for souls opprest,
Nor point them to that place of rest,
From sin and sorrow free.

Love smoothes life's dark and thorny way,
Beguiles the weary hours,
Makes glad the long, the darksome day,
Makes dull November bright as May,
And on our path strews flowers.

Love sweetens life with all its cares,
When pass'd with one we love,
Who all our joys and sorrows shares,
Whose love us saves from many snares,
Who true to us doth prove.

Adieu to earth, to Heaven we turn,
Where Love doth ever reign,
Where its pure flame doth ever burn,
Where cold hearts we shall never mourn,
Nor ever hate again.

Our God is Love! His heart, His name,
And His love changeth never!
Ah, nought can quench its sacred flame,
From age to age it is the same,
It burneth on for ever!

Jesus is Love! for us He died
Upon the bitter tree,
And now He lives to be our Guide,
For all our wants He will provide,
And will our Shepherd be.

The Spirit loves! doth He not plead,
And heav'nly grace impart?
Doth He not for us intercede,
And give us grace in time of need?
He cheers the drooping heart.

The Angels love! to us they come
In sorrow's gloomy day,
They bid the wand'rer no more roam,
They lead the pilgrim to his home,
And cheer him on his way.

Saints also love ! who now on high
　Rejoice before the throne,
They bend on us the watchful eye,
Those ransomed ones may oft be nigh
　When we seem all alone.

All Heaven is Love ! no stormy night
　Can fall on realms above,
For in that home so fair, so bright,
We 'll dwell in Love, and Love is light,
　For God Himself is *Love !*

January 25, 1860.

TRUST IN GOD.

LORD! as the ivy to the oak,
   So would I cling to Thee,
Thou wilt defend me from the storms
   Of bleak adversity.

For Thou wilt be my Strength and Stay,
   When darkness veils my sky;
When tempests rage, and all is gloom,
   I'll feel Thee ever nigh.

When lightnings flash, when thunders roll,
   I will the closer cling,
And calm, confiding, cheerful rest
   Beneath Thy shelt'ring wing.

For Thou my Refuge and my Rock
   In time of need will be;
Thou wilt me save, my gracious God,
   For I do trust in Thee.

Oh! may I ever upwards aim,
   Like to that ivy green,
Which clings to yonder stately oak,
   Which many a storm has seen.

So would I cleave to Thee, my God,
Let nought me from Thee sever,
But may I 'neath Thy shade abide,
Now, henceforth, and for ever!

January 30, 1860.

ON HOPE.

 RIGHT star of Hope! whose cheering ray
Illumes with joy life's darkest day,
For she doth sun my pilgrim way
    When all is dark and drear.

Without her light this world would be
A desert drear, where we should see
No refuge whither we could flee
    When angry storms are near.

Hope points her rainbow in the cloud,
When skies are veiled in thickest shroud,
When winds and waves are raging loud,
    Bright gleams of light appear.

Hope is oft the child of sorrow,
Yet from her we comfort borrow,
For she points to that to-morrow
    Which shall be ever bright.

On future joys with eagle eye
She looks, and soars, then soars more high,
Inciting us from earth to fly
    To yonder land of light.

Her pinions strengthened are by flight ;
She gilds with joy the darkest night,
And silvers with her radiant light,
    Life's weary, lonely way.

Hope ! precious anchor of the soul !
When swelling billows o'er us roll,
And foaming rage, without control,
    'Tis then we own her sway.

Into the Rock of Ages cast,
The chain of Love will hold it fast,
Till, all the raging storms o'erpast,
    We hail the port of peace.

Celestial Hope ! in sorrow near,
To wipe away the falling tear,
And point the mourner to that sphere
    Where all his sorrows cease.

Bright Star ! at death we see her stand,
Her torch bright burning in her hand,
Disclosing yonder spirit-land,
    Beyond the gates of glory.

There Faith and Hope their mission end,
Then back to earth their steps they bend,
To nerve the faint, the sick to tend,
    Till finish'd is life's story.

In yonder land Hope's taper-light
Is needed not, for there's no night,
There Hope is joy, and Faith is sight,
    And all is cloudless day.

Guardian Graces! bright wings of Love!
She drops them at the gates above,
And enters Heaven *alone,* to prove
    That there *Love* reigns for aye!

February 4, 1860.

TO A SNOWDROP.

WEET to see thee, pensive snowdrop,
Blooming in the lonely churchyard,
Bending o'er the graves of loved ones,
As if their precious dust to guard.

Thy tiny petals, spotless, pure,
Do vie in whiteness with the snow,
Drooping so meekly to the ground,
Mourning for those who sleep below.

How we hail thee, lovely flow'ret,
When all around is dark and drear!
Thy coming cheers the mourner's heart,
And bids us dry the falling tear.

Thou point'st us to that blissful morn,
When we, too, from the dead shall rise,
To bloom in loveliness for aye
In realms of love beyond the skies.

Ah! *there* the flow'rets never fade,
No storm can e'er their bloom destroy;
Perpetual spring doth ever reign
In that bright land of peace and joy.

February 13, 1860.

ON THE SNOW.

HOW pure is the snow,
　　Mantling all here below,
With a garment so fair and so bright!
　　How beauteous the trees,
　　As they wave in the breeze,
Clad in robes of so sparkling a white!

　　Thus pure is the soul
　　By Jesus made whole,
And washed in His own precious blood.
　　No sin doth remain,
　　Not a spot, not a stain,
When cleansed in that all-healing flood.

　　Our sins all forgiven,
　　In Him we are hidden,
And in His robe dazzling arrayed.
　　Thus are we all clad,
　　And in Him are glad,
For He hath sin's penalty paid.

　　But sin comes again,
　　Like fierce winds and rain,
And stains that fair mantle of white.
　　Then to Jesus we'll go,
　　He will pardon bestow,
And make our robes shine still more bright.

February 16, 1860.

"SHE HATH DONE WHAT SHE COULD."

MARK XIV. AND VIII., FIRST CLAUSE.

SWEET, precious words ! to Mary spoken,
 By her belovèd Lord,
As He 'neath Simon's favoured roof,
 Sat round the festal board ;
For He was there a welcome guest.
That family, that scene how blest,
 On that auspicious night !
Ah ! never shall forgotten be,
That loving scene in Bethany,
 It was a hallowed sight.

When Mary heard her Lord was there,
 With cheerful heart-felt pleasure,
She hastened to that honoured home,
 With her most precious treasure,
That she her gratitude might prove,
Might give a token of her love
 To Him whom she adored.
The depth of her love who can tell,
For He had raised her when she fell,
 And her to peace restored.

That box of alabaster white,
 With joy she now did open,
And poured the ointment on His head,
 Of her deep love the token.

Indignant some around her said,
" Why was this waste of ointment made ?"
" Why not sold for the poor ?"
But Jesus said, " Let her alone,
This loving deed shall be made known,
    So long as ages 'dure."

" The poor ye alway have with you,
    And ye may do them good;
But *Me* ye have not alway, and
    ' *She* hath done what she could ;'
This work which she on Me hath wrought,
So long as Gospel truths are taught,
    Shall still recorded be;
To many a soul 'twill comfort bring,
'Twill raise it up on hopeful wing
    My grace and love to see."

While some base hearts were murmuring,
    The Lord her deed did praise,
He gave her of His joy to taste,
    And up her thoughts did raise
To that bright home where she would rest,
For ever happy, ever blest,
    Where no sin dare intrude;
Where those sweet words would greet her ear,
Pronounced by Him in accents clear,
    " She hath done what she could."

" She hath done what she could,"—may this
    Be ever said of me,
As daily I, through grace divine,
    Like Jesus strive to be;

Oh ! may I meekly bear my cross,
And count for Him all things but loss
   If only Him I know.
Oh ! may I in His footsteps tread,
Living to God, to this world dead,
   In grace, oh, may I grow !

Oh ! may these words be said of me
   E'en now in this cold world,
Whilst struggling with indwelling sin,
   Whose banner's oft unfurled.
May Jesus aid me in the fight,
Oh ! may I keep mine armour bright
   By earnest, wrestling prayer,
Then in His strength I'll onward go,
Victorious over ev'ry foe,
   Until the crown I wear.

" She hath done what she could,"—may this
   Fall gently on mine ear,
When, at the solemn hour of death,
   My Saviour shall appear,
That He may claim me as His own ;
That I may share His joy, His throne,
   Through bright eternal day,
May sound on golden harp His praise,
Who did my soul from death upraise
   That I might live for aye !

February 24, 1860.

HYMN

ON THE SAME WORDS,

"She hath done what she could."

WHEN groaning 'neath a load of sin,
  When anxious thoughts intrude,
How cheering are those precious words!
  "She hath done what she could."

When mourning mine unworthiness,
  That I do no more good,
How sweet to hear in gentlest tone!
  "She hath done what she could."

In moments of despondency,
  When trust the Lord I would,
How sweet that whisper 'mid the gloom!
  "She hath done what she could."

When men revile me for His sake,
  May harsh thoughts be subdued,
May I bear all, that I may hear
  "She hath done what she could."

When labouring for my blessèd Lord,
  With His own Spirit endued,
Oh! may He cheer me with these words,
  "She hath done what she could."

When treading death's dark dreary vale,
  Should gloomy thoughts intrude,
May softly fall upon mine ear,
  " She hath done what she could."

And when I see Thee in that home,
  Where all are happy, good,
Let these blest words be heard by me,
  " She hath done what she could."

March 1, 1860.

SONNET FOR CHILDREN.

SPRING.

PRING is coming! Spring is coming!
　　With all its flow'rets gay,
　The sweet cuckoo, the sprightly lark,
　　Shall carol their glad lay.

Again shall Nature wake from sleep,
　　And rise from Winter's tomb,
The trees shall bud and blossom gay,
　　The modest violet bloom.

The primrose pale, the cowslip sweet,
　　The crocus of bright hue,
The snowdrop pure, the lily fair,
　　Shall deck our fields anew.

The valleys, clad in vernal green,
　　Shall be a welcome sight,
The balmy gales, the blossoms rich,
　　Shall fill us with delight.

And then we'll see the little lambs
　　A-skipping o'er the lea;
The husbandman will sow the seed,
　　A harvest rich to see.

As gentle Spring, with its sun showers,
　Puts forth its blossoms gay,
So may we in our youth's bright Spring
　Improve each fleeting day.

That so our Summer may be bright,
　Our Autumn richly blest,
Our Winter calm, until we take
　Our peaceful, hopeful rest.

March 10, 1860.

BIRTHDAY HYMN.

 NEW I dedicate myself,
My gracious God, to Thee,
Throughout another year of care
Thou hast sustainèd me.

My heart is filled with gratitude
For all Thy love to me,
Thy tender mercy hath me kept
From ev'ry danger free.

For thou hast been my Hiding-place
When foes were swift and strong,
When clouds and darkness veiled my sky
Thou wast my Shield, my Song.

And shall I see this day again ?
Ah ! thou alone canst tell,
But I'll not fear, I'll trust Thy love,
For Thou dost all things well.

Though suffering has my portion been,
I never will repine,
But meekly kiss the chastening rod,
'Tis needed discipline.

It weans my heart from earthly things,
  And centres it in Heaven,
It is a pledge of Jesus' love,
  To ransomed pilgrims given.

My path through life has thorny been—
  A path of grief and care,
And oft-times have my sorrows been
  Greater than I could bear.

Deep after deep hath past o'er me,
  And billow after billow,
Yet Thou, my Rock, hast ever been
  My soul's calm, peaceful Pillow.

There shall I rest in calm repose
  Through all life's darksome way,
Nought shall I dread, for Thou, my God,
  Shalt be my Strength and Stay.

And when through Jordan's swelling waves
  I pass to yonder shore,
Be Thou, my precious Saviour, near,
  And bid me fear no more.

Then welcome me to Heaven's joys,
  Where I'll Thy glory see,
And praise Thee for Thy grace and love
  Through all eternity.

Oh! let my earnest prayers, my God,
  Be heard this day by Thee,
Then, though my homeward path be dark,
  I'll ever peaceful be.

March 19, 1860.

ACROSTIC.

E ACH day may I more faithful be,
L iving to Him who died for me,
I mproving well life's fleeting day,
Z ealous for Him who is my Stay
A s still I tread this weary way.

S hady, oft dark, my path has been,
A long this dreary desert scene,
W hen waves of sorrow o'er me rolled,
E ver has He their rage controlled,
R est then I will on Jesus' breast,
S ecure from dangers, tranquil, blest.

March 19, 1860.

HAD I THE WINGS OF A GENTLE DOVE.

"Oh ! that I had the wings of a dove ! for then would I
fly away, and be at rest."—*Psalm* lv. 6.

AD I the wings of the gentle dove,
   I'd flee away to my home above,
   Where all is peace, and where all is love,
     Where bliss doth ever reign.

Away from this earth I fain would soar
To Heaven, where sorrow is known no more,
And meet all my loved ones gone before,
     No more to part again.

There, leaning on Jesus' loving breast,
With Him I would taste eternal rest,
No more afflicted, no more opprest,
     But blest, most blest, for aye.

For ah ! in that land of love and light
No tear of sorrow shall dim my sight,
No dark forebodings, no dreary night,
     All *there* is cloudless day.

Soon will the day dawn, night's shadows flee,
Then in bright glory Jesùs I'll see,
Like Him, and with Him evermore be,
     His bliss, His crown will share.

My harp I 'll attune to sound His praise,
I 'll joy in His smile through endless days,
And bask in the light of His cheering rays,
For all is glory *there!*

March 24, 1860.

ACROSTIC.

TO AUNT.

 A Y'ST thou the same high honour claim
A s she who bore that loving name ;
R ich blessings on thy head descend.
Y ea, God from ill shall thee defend.

S o shall thy path be smooth and bright
A mid the gloom of life's dark night,
W hen storms arise then tranquil be,
E ach cloud but whispers, " Trust in Me."
R est, then, on Jesus' gentle breast,
S ecure from harm, for ever blest !

Abril 5, 1860.

TO A LOCK OF HAIR.

THIS day the birth commemorates
 Of one beloved by me,
Of whom thou art remembrancer,
 When her no more I see.

Fair lock! I love to gaze on thee,
 I treasure thee with care,
Memento sad of one that's gone,
 Who was surpassing fair.

Thou dost recall my youthful days,
 Days full of mirth and glee,
When we, light-hearted friends, did meet,
 From care, from sorrow free.

A few short years, how changed the scene!
 Loos'd was the silver cord,
Her spirit soared unto its home,
 The bosom of the Lord.

How peaceful was that bed of death!
 She calmly fell asleep,
For Jesus in that hour her soul
 In perfect peace did keep.

And now she gems the Saviour's crown,
   Her sins are all forgiven,
She reigns, a happy ransomed one,
   Amid the choir of Heaven.

Yet oft, methinks, that loving voice
   Falls softly on mine ear,
As I was wont in days gone by
   Its merry tones to hear.

She was so joyous, yet so meek,
   So gentle, loving, kind,
That when I look on thee it doth
   Bring happy days to mind.

But oh ! I will not selfish be,
   For she is happy, blest,
She's free from sin, and now doth rest
   On Jesus' loving breast.

Much as I miss that faithful friend,
   I would not her recall,
Ah ! no, for she is happier far ,
   Her Saviour's now her *All.*

Then, precious lock, I'll guard thee well,
   And as I gaze on thee,
I'll think of her whose once thou wast,
   And who was loved by me.

April 14, 1860.

ACROSTIC.

TO TOM.

T O thee, my son, these lines are penned,
H appy mayst thou ever be ;
O n this thy happy natal day
M ay a blessing rest on thee ;
A s in years, in wisdom grow,
S mooth thy path be here below.

S ixteen summers hast thou seen,
A nd they all have sunny been,
W hat's before thee none can know,
E ach day will its strength bestow,
R esist the snares around thee laid,
S erve the Lord, in sun or shade.

M ay many happy years be thine,
I f it be the will Divine ;
T rust in God with all thine heart,
C hoose the good, the better part.
H appy, then, thy path will be,
E 'n though clouds thou ofttimes see,
L et thy Saviour be thy light,
L ife's day, then, will all be bright !

April 17, 1860.

SPRING FLOWERS.

PRING flow'rets have a charm for me,
  A charm too deep to tell,
  They o'er my weary, aching heart
  Exert a magic spell.

For, as I gaze upon these flowers,
  So exquisitely fair,
I think of Jesus' mighty power,
  Of Jesus' love and care.

The lowly lily of the vale,
  The crocus of gay hue,
The primrose, the hepatica,
  The modest violet blue.

All these, and many, many more,
  Now deck our parterres gay,
How lovely are their varied tints !
  How fair their bright array !

A few months since where were those flowers ?
  Deep buried in the earth,
Awaiting spring's glad, welcome step,
  Anew to give them birth.

And 'twill be so with us when we
  Shall slumber in the tomb,
The joyous resurrection morn
  Dispel shall winter's gloom,

And we shall wake from death's long sleep,
  To fade, ah ! nevermore,
But through an endless spring to bloom,
  Life's wintry storms all o'er.

Then hail ! fair children of the spring,
  So lovely, bright, and gay,
Short-lived and fading though ye be,
  Ye 'll bloom your little day.

And if my God so cares for you,
  Ah ! how much more for me,
He will me love, me save and keep,
  My Hope, my Life will be.

April 21, 1860.

ACROSTIC.

TO ELIZABETH.

ARNEST in all that's great and good,
L et no dark gloomy thoughts intrude,
I mprove each golden, fleeting day,
Z ealous for Christ, "the Life, the Way,"
A h! live to God, He is thy Stay,
B ut should dark clouds bedim thy sky,
E 'en through the gloom lift up thine eye,
T ear-dimmed, ah, yes! though oft it be,
H ath He not whisper'd, " Cling to Me."

P ensive and sad thou ofttimes art,
A s days gone by steal o'er thine heart,
T urn in that hour to Jesus' breast,
E 'en as thou look'st, He'll give thee rest,
R eposing there, thou'lt peaceful be,
S unshine nor shade shall move not thee,
O h, no! life's stream shall tranquil flow,
N ought shall e'er mar its course below.

P ursue thy lone, but onward way,
A nd soon 'twill end in brightest day,
T here may we meet around God's throne,
O nce in that bright, that happy home,
N o sin, no death, shall e'er be known.

S o may it be, my own dear friend,
A nd may God's love thy steps attend,
W ork, watch, and pray, ne'er daunted be,
E ach day will strength be given to thee,
R est in the Lord, trust in Him ever!
S o shall thy path be weary never!

April 26, 1860.

STANZA.

ON BEAUTY.

WHAT is beauty external? a perishing
flower,
Which like to the cistus may fade in
an hour.
But what's beauty mental? a tree evergreen,
Whose blossoms enliven this dark, dreary scene ;
Oh ! may we possess it, 'twill ne'er know decay,
'Tis like to the amaranth, ne'er fading away.

April 30, 1860.

TO A FRIEND.

REMEMBER me at dawn of day,
Oh ! let thy thoughts to me oft stray,
And then with joy I 'll think of thee,
For I will know thou think'st of me.

Remember me throughout the day,
While treading life's oft weary way,
Fond, kindred hearts nought e'er shall sever,
True, true they will remain for ever !

Remember me at evening bright,
Ere fall the dusky shades of night,
Though sunder'd far, in thought we 'll meet,
And each the other fondly greet.

Remember me at midnight hour,
May Heaven its blessings on thee shower,
Then, till we meet, O think of me,
And I will aye remember thee.

May 11, 1860.

RESPONSE TO THE FOREGOING.

FORGET thee I will not, to me thou art dear,
On my heart deep engraved, when far as
when near ;
I'll love thee in sorrow, when all's dark as
night,
I'll love thee in sunshine, when all's calm and bright.

Forget thee I will not, at morn, noon, and night,
I'll think of thee alway, with heart-felt delight,
Though absent in person, still present in thought,
Though distance divide us, thou'lt ne'er be forgot.

Forget thee I will not, ah, no! this fond heart
Shall cherish and love thee, nought, nought shall us part ;
True and faithful we'll be through life's little while,
Our path alway cheered by love's gladsome smile.

Forget thee I will not, though we ne'er meet again,
In this heart I will guard thee, there, there thou shalt
reign,
Thee will I remember till life's latest day,
Nought, nought shall e'er-tear thee from this heart
away !

May 19, 1860.

ON THE BREEZE.

EAREST thou the gentle breeze
Playing 'mong the leafy trees,
In this merry month of May,
When all Nature's bright and gay?

Hearest thou its cheerful sound
Giving life to all around?
Sporting on the breast of ocean,
Setting all its waves in motion.

Balmy is the southern breeze,
Sighing softly 'mongst the trees,
Healthful is the western gale,
As we roam the verdant vale.

Insects dance mid-way in air,
Flow'rets blossom rich and fair,
Larks and blackbirds sweetly sing,
Joyous, woods and valleys ring.

Bathed in sunshine is the scene,
Trees and fields are clad in green,
Mountains, brooklets, all are glad,
Making sad hearts feel less sad.

But it is not alway so,
For when eastern winds do blow
Nature wears a mournful shroud,
All is mist, and gloom, and cloud.

And when chilling Boreas howls,
When the sky with blackness scowls,
Then we long for balmy gales,
Then we sigh for sunlit vales.

Yet the sunshine cannot last,
Swift the sky is overcast,
Now the sun, and now the shade,
Now we bloom, and then we fade.

Pleasing is variety,
Constant sun would dazzling be,
Doth he not appear more bright
After clouds as dark as night?

As the breeze, so sweetly soft,
Raises drooping hearts aloft,
So the Spirit gently gladdens
Hearts that bitter sorrow saddens.

May 25, 1860.

ACROSTIC.

TO MARY.

 AYST thou see many happy years,
A lthough thou tread'st a vale of tears,
R emember life is but a day,
Y outh's pleasures all shall pass away.

S erene and sunny be thy life
A mid this scene of care and strife;
W hen shadows flit across thy sky,
E 'en in the gloom lift up thine eye,
R adiant with hope the clouds will be,
S ilv'ry linings they'll have to thee.

M ay hope, on this thy natal day,
I ts flow'rets strew upon thy way;
T hough ofttimes gloomy it may be,
C herish bright hope, and clouds will flee.
H ope on, hope ever, patient wait,
E re long be thine a happy fate,
L ove's banner wave shall o'er thy way,
L ife then will be a summer's day.

June 1, 1860.

TO A SPRIG OF VERBENA.

WEET, fragrant sprig! culled by a friend,
    Thou 'rt treasured up with care,
Preserved by me thou still shalt be,
    For thou to me art fair.

For thou didst bloom, sweet, lovely flower,
    In Arran's sunny Isle,
Close by a little cottage door
    Thou blossomed for a while.

Till, sever'd from thy parent stem,
    To me thou wert consigned,
That thou mightst, by thy sweet perfume,
    Keep happy days in mind.

And where is now that parent stem?
    Cut down and left to die;
And where the friend of that sweet cot?
    Safe in his home on high.

But I shall treasure thee, fair flower,
    Thou precious art to me,
Thou dost recall that happy friend
    Who loved and cherish'd thee.

But now that pretty cot and all
   Are levelled with the ground,
Nought, nought remains to mark the spot,
   All, all is still around.

For nought but verdure decks that spot
   Where grew those lovely flowers,
All, all have past, as sparkling dew,
   Or Summer's gentle showers.

Yes, all are gone ! that faithful friend,
   Those flowers, those trees, that cot,
All are as if they 'd never been,
   By many a one forgot.

Yet not by me, ah ! no, that friend
   Shall ne'er forgotten be,
That cottage with its flowers, all, all
   Shall live in memory.

June 4, 1860.

ACROSTIC.

TO COUSIN ISABELLA.

 WISH thee joy this happy day,
S mooth be thine upward, onward way,
A nd as life's day is fleeting fast,
B e thou, then, faithful to the last.
E ach day improve; in light or shade,
L et thy heart on the Lord be stayed,
L ook unto Him, who sweetly said,
" A h! it is I, be not afraid."

S o shall thy path be calm, serene,
A mid this dreary pilgrim scene;
W hen darksome clouds o'ercast thy sky,
E 'en through the gloom lift up thine eye,
R ainbow'd with love they'll be to thee,
S weet, then, to hear, " Cling, cling to Me."

M ay many happy years be thine,
A nd should clouds come, do not repine;
C onfide in Him whose name is Love,
P rovide He will, thy fears remove;
H appy then be, and peaceful rest,
E 'en though ofttimes by cares opprest;
R epose in Jesus, list His voice,
" S till trust My love, in Me rejoice,"
O h! then, on this thy natal day,
N ought need distress thee on thy way.

June 7, 1860.

F

FAREWELL.

 WORD in faltering accents breathed,
　　When friend from friend doth part,
Which brings a tear to many an eye,
　　A pang to many a heart.

For as we whisper that sad word,
　　Does not the thought steal o'er us,
We may not see those friends again,
　　The future's dark before us.

They go across the stormy main,
　　Unto an alien land,
They leave their country, friends, all, all,
　　At duty's stern command.

What dangers may await them there,
　　What ills may them betide,
Alas! we know not, but we know
　　They have a faithful Guide.

But as we speak that word "Farewell,"
　　We also breathe the prayer,
That God would bless those lovèd ones,
　　Be with them everywhere.

Replete with sadness is that word,
  It speaks of days gone by,
Bright, happy days, which only now
  Can live in memory.

Though sunder'd far from those dear friends,
  We will forget them never!
For love doth closely bind our hearts,
  . Nought, nought shall e'er them sever.

Then ever as we say "Farewell,"
  With a thoughtful, glist'ning eye,
We'll bear in mind that we'll all meet
  In our home beyond the sky.

No farewells there! such mournful words
  Can rend our hearts, ah! never,
The parting tear, the last embrace,
  Are known no more for ever!

June 16, 1860.

RUTH AND NAOMI.

HOW touching are the words of Ruth!
How full of sympathy!
Her aged friend she would not leave,
But to her she did fondly cleave,
Close, heav'nly was the tie.

"Oh! entreat me not to leave thee,"
Said she with tearful eye,
"Where'er thou goest I will go,
Nought e'er shall part us here below,
Forsake thee will not I.

"For where thou lodgest I will lodge,
Thy God *my* God shall be,
Thy people, country, shall be mine,
Henceforth I'll dwell with thee and thine,
Till death part thee and me."

A bright example this of love,
Of faith and constancy,
Ruth did fulfil a daughter's part,
She loved and clung with all her heart
To aged Naomi.

How deep, how lasting was that love !
May I as faithful be
To Thee, O Jesus ! may I cleave,
For Thou wilt never, never leave
The soul that clings to Thee.

All through this weary desert scene
Thou wilt be near to me,
When all alone, I'll feel Thee nigh
To list my prayer, to mark my sigh,
My Strength, my Stay to be.

June 24, 1860.

AN ONLY CHILD.

"I WISH I were an only child,
　　Then I would happy be,
My father's care, my mother's love
　　Would lavished be on me.

" No brothers rude would me molest,
　　No sisters me annoy,
Then would my days all pleasant be,
　　My life a scene of joy."

Thus spake a little child to me,
　　Whilst heavily she sighed,
And looked at me with tearful eyes,
　　To whom I thus replied—

" Ah ! speak not so, my little one,
　　Ye know not what ye say,
'Tis sad to be an only child,
　　Alone from day to day.

" No brothers kind, no sisters dear,
　　Thy griefs, thy joys to share,
All, all alone, thy little cares
　　And sorrows thou must bear.

" Ye may a loving mother have,
A father, tender, kind,
Yet thou wouldst miss a kindred friend
To unbosom all thy mind.

" Then wish not, oh ! my little child,
Thou wert an only one,
For ah ! it is a heartless thing
To feel so all alone.

" Then happy, grateful ever be
That gentle hearts thee love,
That brothers dear, and sisters kind,
Around thy pathway move.

" They 'll smooth the rugged path of life,
And cheer thee when thou 'rt sad,
They 'll lighten all thy little cares,
And make thy lone heart glad.

" And when shall come the hour of death,
Oh ! think of Heaven above,
And pray that ye may all meet there,
A family of love."

June 30, 1860.

ON *A TEAR.*

HAT is a tear ? a tiny drop,
When shattered is some earthly prop,
Seen glistering in the mournful eye,
Demanding deepest sympathy.

Those tear-drops speak of grief and woe,
As down the cheek they silent flow;
And cold indeed must be that heart
That does not cheering words impart.

This world is but a vale of tears,
Of gloomy doubts, harassing fears :
Tear upon tear doth swiftly flow,
All, all is sorrow here below.

Yet, now and then a tear of joy
(But ah ! 'tis ne'er without alloy),
May glisten in the sunny eye,
When some fond cherish'd friend is nigh.

This is but an oasis green
In this dark, gloomy, chequered scene,
A sunny spot, where soon the cloud
Wraps all again in darkest shroud.

When the heart's with anguish riven,
When from earthly stays we're driven,
Oh, may we closely cling to God,
And humbly, meekly, kiss the rod.

When crushed beneath perplexing fears,
How soothing is a flood of tears!
We'll lean in faith on Jesus' breast,
He'll dry the tear, He'll give us rest.

And when we reach our home on high,
He'll wipe the tear from ev'ry eye ;
For, in that land of perfect joy,
No griefs can e'er our bliss destroy!

July 5, 1860.

THE GRAVE.

THOU swallowest thousands day by day,
   Thou all devouring grave !
None shall escape thy dreaded clasp
   None us from thee can save.

Within thy precincts dark and drear,
   Where lie the countless dead,
Sooner or later we must rest
   In that cold, narrow bed.

All, all must be a prey to thee,
   Each child of human race ;
The rich, the poor, the young, the old,
   Must rest in thine embrace.

Death keeps the key, none him elude,
   To each one he will come,
The messenger of peace to some
   To call their spirits home.

To they who fall asleep in Christ
   He is a welcome friend,
He sends them to their happy home
   Where all their sorrows end.

But ah ! he is the king of terrors
  To all who Christ deny,
Who live as if their rest was here,
  Who think they ne'er shall die.

And where shall be our lowly grave ?
  In yon sweet cemet'ry
Where wave the cypress and the yew,
  Where weeps the willow-tree ?

Where flow'rets bloom, and all is fair ?
  Ah ! no, it may not be ;
We may sleep in a foreign land,
  Or in the deep blue sea.

It matters not : we'll rest in hope
  In our dark, lowly bed,
Until the awful trumpet peals
  To wake the sleeping dead.

Then shall we wake from death's long sleep,
  To live for evermore,
In endless weal or endless woe,
  To taste of death no more.

For Jesus triumphed o'er the grave,
  Then may we sweetly sing,
"O grave ! where is thy vict'ry now,
  And where, O death ! thy sting ?"

July 11, 1860.

TO-DAY.

O-DAY 'S a type of human life,
A scene of toil, of care, of strife,
The dawn of morning may be bright,
The noon-day calm, the evening light.

Yet, ah ! how oft it is not so,
" Changing" is stamped on all below ;
How oft a morn all sunny, bright,
Ere noon-day comes is dark as night.

Cloud upon cloud o'ercasts the sky,
The sea is raging mountains high,
The wind is howling o'er the plain,
In fearful torrents falls the rain.

All, all is gloom ; when suddenly
The storm doth cease, and in the sky
The covenant-bow of peace is seen,
Then, ah ! how changèd is the scene !

The wind is hushed, calm is the sea,
The sun shines out so cheerfully,
And, ere the gentle eventide,
No trace of tempest doth abide.

All, all is still, serenely bright,
Ere fall the dusky shades of night,
When all are wrapt in hopeful sleep,
Whilst stars o'er us their vigils keep.

Ah ! thus it is with our life's day,
Youth's morning may be bright and gay,
Joyous and happy it may be,
From cares, from toils, from sorrows free.

Hope with gay flow'rets strews our way,
Yet oft they droop and fade away,
Then manhood comes with all its cares,
Its sore temptations, many snares.

The world, sin, Satan, all conspire
To shake our faith, and us inspire
With hard and gloomy thoughts of God,
Who makes us tread that thorny road.

Yet, we resist them, bid them flee,
Then all is calm tranquillity;
Our life flows on, a lucid stream,
A pleasant, though a fleeting dream.

And when life's day draws to a close,
Oh! may we lean in sweet repose
On Jesus' gentle, loving breast,
Awaiting calm our peaceful rest.

And when death seals our closing eye,
We'll ope it in our home on high,
Where all's one bright eternal day,
Where shadows all have fled away!

July 19, 1860.

ON ABSENCE.

S there such a thing as "absence"
　　To the fond, the loving heart?
　　Can forgotten be our loved ones?
　　Kindred hearts can aught e'er part?

Ah! no, though friends be sunder'd far,
　　Though vast oceans them divide,
In spirit they are alway near,
　　Faith beholds them at our side.

They mingle in our ev'ry thought,
　　All our joys and sorrows share,
Where'er we are we think of them,
　　And each other's burdens bear.

And is there not one hallow'd spot,
　　Where the sever'd love to meet?
Ah! yes, before the Throne of Grace
　　They can hold communion sweet.

God deigns to meet them there, to list
　　Their mutual fervent prayers,
He will their hearts' desires fulfil,
　　He will lighten all their cares.

'Tis thus God tries His children's faith,
　That they close to Him may cling,
And that they to His throne each friend
　In the arms of faith may bring.

And if it be for good to them,
　They shall meet again in peace,
To tread life's pathway hand in hand,
　Until all their conflicts cease.

But should they meet not here again,
　May they meet in Heaven above,
Where " absence " is a word unknown,
　Where they 'll dwell in perfect love.

July 24, 1860.

ACROSTIC.

TO A FRIEND.

GOD bless thee on thy natal day,
E re thou resume thy pilgrim way ;
O may He in each trying hour
R ichest blessings on thee shower.
G o thou on, Heaven's joys are thine,
E ndless love shall on thee shine.

R ejoice thou in the Lord alway,
U pon Him lean, He is thy Stay,
L ift up thine heart in constant prayer,
E re long thou shalt His glory share

July 30, 1860.

THE SOLDIER'S ADIEU.

AH! must I leave my native land,
   And seek an alien shore?
   And must I quit my home, perchance
   To see it never more?

Yes, I must leave thee, dear loved Isle,
   'Tis duty's stern command,
A soldier's vow is to obey,
   And fight with dauntless hand.

I go to quell the oppressing foe,
   To a far distant land,
But if I'm spared, soon I'll return
   To Britain's peaceful strand.

For I do love my native land,
   Its verdant meads and vales,
Its mountains wild, its brooklets clear,
   Its lovely hills and dales.

But is my home all I've to leave?
   Oh! no, there's many a one
Dear to my heart, and who will think
   On me when I am gone.

But home, and country, friends, to all
  I bid a long adieu,
Yet, as I roam in foreign lands,
  My heart shall be with you.

Sweet thoughts of you shall nerve my hand
  Amid the din of war,
The foeman's spear I will not fear;
  I'll see you from afar.

And if my life shall sparèd be,
  With joy shall I return,
And hail again my native land,
  My friends for whom I mourn.

But should I fall on battlefield,
  My latest prayer shall be,
That God would bless my country, friends,
  That ne'er again I'll see.

Then, sea-girt Isle, land of my birth,
  And friends beloved by me,
I bid ye all adieu, yet still
  Ye'll live in memory.

ARRAN, *August* 5, 1860.

THE SOLDIER'S RETURN.

YEARS rollèd on, from that dear friend
   No tidings ever came,
Day after day we looked in vain
   For that belovèd name.

At length we heard the war was o'er,
   That thousands of the brave
Had fallen in that dark bloody fray,
   And found a warrior's grave.

With anxious mien and beating heart,
   The mournful list we read,
Of those brave sons, who for our cause
   Lay number'd with the dead.

His was not there!   Does he still live?
   Oh! with a grateful heart
We thanked our God, and pondered o'er
   That night when we did part.

His last kind looks, his parting words,
   Rushed back to memory,
And whilst on days gone by we thought,
   A tear bedimmed our eye.

Time passèd on, yet came he not,
  Our hopes seemed blasted, gone,
We spoke of him as one that was,
  Whose earthly race was run.

When lo! one winter's eve, as we
  Sat round the blazing hearth,
Speaking of happy days now gone,
  When he joined in our mirth.

A well-known welcome step drew nigh,
  A well-known voice was heard,
Looks with each other we exchanged,
  Yet uttered not a word.

'Twas he! our long-lost lovèd one,
  Returned to his dear home,
There to enjoy peace, happiness—
  No more from it to roam.

Sweet was the hymn we sang that night,
  And sweet our evening prayer,
As God anew we blessed and thanked
  For His protecting care.

ARRAN, *August* 7, 1860.

"*THEN ALL THE DISCIPLES FORSOOK HIM AND FLED.*"

MATTHEW XXVI. 56, LAST CLAUSE.

HOW sad the thought that in that hour
  The Saviour was alone!
That when He looked for sympathy,
  Lo! ev'ry one was gone,
Of those devoted followers
  There now remained *not one !*

Where was now the fearless Peter?
  Or where the loving John,
Who only a few hours before
  Had leant His breast upon?
Ah! where were they, and all the rest?
  All, all had fled and gone!

Ah! cruel, faithless, coward band,
  How could ye from Him flee?
He who had been so kind to you,
  How could ye traitors be?
How could ye thus forsake your Lord,
  His grief how could ye see?

And is it not still oft the case
  With those who name His name?
Do they not oft deny their Lord,
  Him put to open shame?
Do they not oft reject His grace,
  His love do not proclaim?

Ah ! yes, when all is calm and bright
   From Him they ofttimes fly,
And seek their happiness on earth,
   Forgetting death is nigh
To cut them down, and usher them
   Into eternity.

Yet there are some who to Him cleave
   In sorrow's dreary night,
E'en when misfortune o'er their path
   Has cast its withering blight,
Who trust and rest in Him, and thus
   Their pathway's calm and bright.

And do not friends ofttimes prove cold,
   And turn from us away,
When hopes are blasted, sunshine gone,
   Does not their love decay ?
Their cold neglect, their silent scorn,
   Fill us with sad dismay.

But there are aye a faithful few
   Who never will us leave,
Who, e'en in stern adversity
   Will to us fondly cleave,
Who still with us will sympathise,
   Who ne'er will us deceive.

But oh ! with Jesus 'twas not so,
   He had not one firm friend,
Fearful and faithless were they all,
   Not one their aid would lend,
They fled from Him in that dark hour—
   How this His heart would rend !

But still He meekly bore His woes,
  No suff'rings could Him move,
For us He groaned, He bled, He died,
  So wondrous was His love,
That He from death might us redeem,
  And raise to Heaven above.

Then let us alway to Him cling,
  May we deny Him never,
Nor sun, nor shade, nor calm, nor storm,
  Let nought Him from us sever,
But may we live and reign with Him,
  For ever and for ever!

ARRAN, *August* 13, 1860.

ON THE SEA SHORE.

LONG fair Brodick's pebbly beach I love
alone to stray,
And ponder over bygone days, o'er loved
ones passed away.

I love to sit, wrapt in deep thought, on that calm tranquil shore,
And on devotion's placid wingto Heaven I love to soar.

To hold communion with the skies, to leave the world
behind,
And, as I muse on heavenly things, enjoyment deep I
find.

I close mine eyes on earthly scenes, and there, unseen,
unknown,
I join the bright, the angel throng, in praise around the
throne.

No ear, save Jesus' gracious ear, mine earnest prayers
can hear,
No eye, save His own loving eye, can mark my silent
tear.

'Tis sweet to feel alone with Him, ah ! yes, all, all alone,
To pour out my whole soul in prayer, and all my griefs
make known.

And as I lose myself in Him, earth fadeth quite away,
I rest me in the arms of love, in realms of brightest day.

Yet, ah! this may not alway be, this deep rest may not
  last,
A murmur low falls on mine ear, the vision bright is past.

Ah! 'tis the gentle wavelet, kissing the peaceful strand,
Recalling me to earth again from that bright spirit-land.

How precious are those Pisgah views! they cheer my
  pilgrim way,
'' Excelsior, excelsior," methinks I hear them say.

Thus nerved, back to the busy world with cheerful heart
  I go,
For God is with me, and He will His strength on me
  bestow.

I will not fear its many snares, its scenes of toil and
  strife,
For God will keep my soul in peace, will be my Joy,
  my Life!

ARRAN, *August* 20, 1860.

TO THE EVENING STAR.

AIL ! lovely star of evening,
　How beauteous is thy ray !
　Fondly I love to gaze on thee,
　As fadeth light away.

As darkness deepens o'er the earth,
　More brilliant is thy light,
Calm, shining with thy silvery ray,
　Enlivening each dark night.

Methinks I hear thee sweetly say,
　" Oh ! fix thy thoughts on high,
Set not thine heart on things of earth,
　Mount, mount to this bright sky."

Yet ofttimes darkness shrouds the sky,
　And veils thee from our sight,
In vain we look and gaze for thee,
　Gone is thy presence bright.

We pause awhile, then gaze anew,
　The dark clouds pass away,
Again we hail thee with delight,
　Admire thy cheering ray.

And is it not oft so with us,
  In unbelief's dark night,
God hides His face, and all is gloom,
  Clouds hide Him from our sight?

But Jesus comes! clouds vanish all,.
  He says, " Believe in Me,
I am the bright, the Morning Star,
  My peace I give to thee."

Then all is bright within our souls,
  Calmed is the troubled breast,
We gaze on Him, and all is peace,
  Our weary souls find rest.

Then oh! shine on, bright star of rest,
  And lure our hearts above,
For we in thee behold a type
  Of Him, whose heart is Love!

ARRAN, *August* 27, 1860.

ON THE HILLS.

 LOVE to gaze upon the hills,
    Whose summits tower to Heaven,
They point my soul to yonder land
    Where sins are all forgiven.

They tell me of God's faithfulness,
    His goodness, and His love,
They bid me think of Jesus' care,
    And waft my thoughts above.

For, list to His own gracious words,
    "The mountains *shall* depart,
The everlasting hills be moved,
    Yet loved by Me thou art:

" My love from thee shall ne'er depart,
    I mercy have on thee.
Nor shall the covenant of my peace
    Removèd ever be."

On those sweet, precious promises
    I stay my weary soul,
And when with anxious cares o'erwhelmed,
    Those hills my fears control.

And as they rear their lofty peaks
　To catch the dews of Heaven,
So, to the soul that soars aloft,
　Shall God's blest Spirit be given.

When tempests rise, like to those hills
　I ne'er shall movèd be,
The storm may beat, the winds may howl,
　I'll look on tranquilly.

And when I climb some Pisgah height,
　A Pisgah view be mine,
There may I bask 'neath Jesus' love,
　May His face on me shine.

ARRAN, *Sept.* 1, 1860.

ON THE SEA-BIRD.

OST thou see that lovely sea-bird,
Calm resting on the crested billow ?
So would I lean on Jesus' breast,
My weary soul's calm, peaceful pillow.

Scarce will it touch these foaming waves,
It only skims them with its wings,
So would I shun temptation's snares,
And loosely sit to earthly things.

And when those heaving billows swell,
It calmly sits, it knows no fear,
Why should it dread the tempest's rage
When it doth know a shelter 's near ?

For, let us trace it in its flight
To yonder rock where is its nest,
There calm it sits, and views the storm,
No fear stirs in its peaceful breast.

And with the Christian it is so,
He feels His Father alway nigh,
And flees to His fond, loving breast,
When dark and lowering is his sky.

Kept as the apple of *His* eye,
Who marks each look, each prayer, each tear,
And, circled by His arms of love,
He knows no shadow of a fear.

Hid in the cleft of Christ, his Rock,
He smiles at dangers, tempests, all,
O'ershadowed by that shelter sweet,
No storm can e'er his soul appal.

ARRAN, *Sept.* 10, 1860.

ACROSTIC

TO UNCLE.

HE Lord thee bless this happy day,
H ope gilds with light thy pilgrim way,
O may love on thy path still shine,
M ay many tranquil years be thine.
A t eventide may it be light,
S o shall thy life be tranquil, bright.

S hade has with sunshine mingled been,
A mid this changing chequered scene,
W hen clouds have dimmed thy sunny sky,
E 'en 'mid the gloom thou could'st descry
R ays of bright hope to cheer thee on,
S till trust till pilgrim days are done.

ARRAN, *Sept.* 16, 1860.

ON THE TWILIGHT.

HOW sweet the solemn twilight hour !
  'Tis then I love to stray
By pebbly beach or heath-clad hill,
  To muse, to praise, to pray.

All is so tranquil and serene,
  I feel that God is nigh,
To hear my lowly earnest prayers,
  To list mine ev'ry sigh.

All Nature rests in calm repose,
  All, all is hushed and still,
For not a sound is heard around
  Save the sweet rippling rill.

Reminding me that thus life flows,
  That time doth ever fly,
Me bearing on untiring wing
  To my blest home on high.

The little flow'rets are asleep,
  Set is the orb of day,
The feathered songsters of the grove,
  Sung have their evening lay.

And all is still as death, no sound
  Falls on the listening ear,
Save the faint sighs of yonder brook,
  Meandering crystal clear.

I think then of that solemn time
  When I shall fall asleep,
May Jesus, in that hour, my soul
  In peace, in safety keep.

Then shall I wake in that bright land,
  Where twilight entereth never !
Where all is bright, eternal day,
  For ever and for ever !

ARRAN, *Sept.* 20, 1860.

ON SHELLS.

 LOVE to wander on the beach,
   And list the billows roar,
I love to see the little shells
   Strewed on the lovely shore.

Sweet treasures of the mighty deep,
   The prey of ocean's storms,
How exquisitely fair are ye !
   How varied are your forms !

Bright, beauteous gems of ocean,
   Dear, dear are ye to me,
In you a loving Father's hand
   And mighty power I see.

In infancy 'twas my delight
   To search the fruitful shore,
And treasure up these little shells,
   Their secret nooks explore.

And though these youthful days are past,
   Forgot they ne'er shall be,
To memory they are present oft,
   They cherished are by me.

And still I love those tiny gems
  That deck the beauteous shore,
I love, I love to gather them,
  Although a child no more.

I love at morn, at noon, at night,
  To roam about the beach,
For those fair treasures of the deep
  Some truths most precious teach.

They prove to me that God is good,
  A God of love is He,
Who for such tiny creatures cares,
  Will He not care for me ?

Ah, yes ! as I those gems pick up,
  God's goodness I'll adore,
I'll lift my heart in silent prayer,
  Be fearful nevermore !

ARRAN, *Sept.* 23, 1860.

ON THE DEW.

H ! seest thou that sparkling gem
Fit for a monarch's diadem,
Glittering on that rose-bud fair,
At evening's calm, how came it there ?

Ah ! 'tis the precious gift of Heaven,
Unto this earth in mercy given,
Descending gently over all,
So soft that scarce you see it fall.

Glad, glad is now the parchèd ground,
Diffused is freshness all around,
Its blest effects may now be seen,
All Nature's decked in brighter green.

The flow'rets now refreshed, repose,
Their tiny, lovely petals close,
Until the morrow's sun shall rise
And bid them ope their little eyes.

Thus doth the Spirit joy impart
To many a weary, drooping heart,
When struggling 'neath the woes of life
He comes and fits us for the strife.

When crushed beneath the weight of sin,
With foes without and fears within,
He loves to pour the healing balm,
He points us to the bleeding Lamb.

And when life's day is dark and dreary,
Or when our nights are long and weary,
He comes to dry the mourner's tears,
His presence soothes, revives, and cheers.

And when shall come death's solemn hour,
We'll fall asleep, like that sweet flower,
To wake and bloom 'neath yon bright sky,
Where flow'rets ne'er shall fade nor die.

ARRAN, *Sept.* 28, 1860.

VERSES ON WILD FLOWERS.

E bloomed beneath a sunny sky
    In lovely Arran Isle,
  We grew in beauty and in grace,
    We flourished for a while;
Till, culled by some fair, gentle hand,
    We treasured were with care,
For, ah! in loveliness of form,
    What can with us compare?

Will not He who so lovingly careth for us,
    Who do droop, fade, and die in a day,
Much more care for, protect, and watch over thee
    Who shall dwell in His presence for aye?

Ye beauteous flow'rets of the field,
    So lovely, sweet, and fair!
  In you we see a Father's love,
    And trace a Father's care.

How can we fail to love you, ye gentle little flowers,
Who so gracefully and sweetly adorn our garden bowers,
Where we are wont to go alone, to commune with our
    God,
To pour our souls into His ear, to read His holy Word.

Can not He who for us careth,
  Watch also over thee?
Then why afraid? thou faithless one,
  The Lord thy Shield shall be.

We bloomed in lovely Arran Isle
  Beneath a cloudless sky,
And now we are preserved with care
  To please the youthful eye.
In us you see the hand of love,
  How beauteous is our hue!
How lovely are our varied tints,
  As we now meet your view!

October 2, 1860.

ACROSTIC.

TO COUSIN MARY.

AY days of sunshine yet be thine,
A nd happy mayst thou be,
R edeem the time, it fleets away,
Y es, days and years swift flee.

S ilent, ah ! silently they glide,
A down life's rapid stream,
W hilst we, unconscious of its speed,
E ach day pass as a dream,
R un, then, with speed the onward race,
S trengthened by love, and nerved by grace.

M ay God thee bless this happy day,
A nd hear thee as ye pray,
C ause shine on thee His blessed face,
P reserve thee day by day;
H ow cheerful then thou mayest be,
E 'en though thy path be drear,
R est in the Lord, and on Him wait,
S hall He not banish fear ?
O h ! then, Him trust, and seek His face,
N e'er, ne'er shall He deny thee grace.

October 9, 1860.

HIDDEN ONES.

GOD'S hidden ones! ah! who are they?
Children of light and of the day,
The lowly contrite ones, whose love
Is fixed on God and things above.

God's hidden ones! ah! where are they?
Not 'mid the rich, the great, the gay,
But in some lonely, humble spot,
There God, our God, forgets them not.

God's hidden ones! ah! what are they?
The scorn of men, to grief a prey,
Yet sons of God, and heirs of grace,
They rest in peace in His embrace.

God's hidden ones! what shall they be?
His kings and priests eternally;
With Him in glory they shall reign,
Nor ever taste of death again.

God's hidden ones! ah! name how blest!
Ye now in Jesus' bosom rest;
Hereafter ye shall all be known,
And joy for aye before the throne.

God's hidden ones ! then do not fear
Though life be dreary, He is near,
His smile shall gild the darkest day,
His hand shall wipe each tear away.

God's hidden ones ! though lonely now,
Ere long the crown shall wreathe your brow ;
Ye'er nearing home, then cheerful be,
For soon ye shall His glory see.

God's hidden ones ! oh ! think of this,
Ye'll be like Him in perfect bliss,
Ne'ermore shall tears bedim your eye
In your bright home beyond the sky.

October 12, 1860.

HYMN

H! make me, holy Father,
  Thy gentle, loving child,
Like to my precious Saviour,
  Meek, holy, pure, and mild.

Oh! may I love Thee more,
  Thee follow day by day,
Then shall I never wander
  From wisdom's heavenly way.

In sorrow's gloomy day,
  May I cling close to Thee,
For Thou my Strength, my Stay,
  My Hope, my Sun, shalt be.

When all around is night,
  When life is dark and drear,
Be Thou my shining light,
  O Jesus, be *Thou* near,

To whisper soothing words,
  To cheer my lonely heart,
And to my wounded soul
  Thy healing balm impart.

For I am ofttimes sad,
  By anguish deep opprest,
Then let me, Jesus, lean,
  Calm pillowed on Thy breast.

There I would ever rest,
  Till face to face I see
The loved one of my soul,
  And like Him holy be.

Let this bright hope me cheer,
  Sustain my bleeding heart,
That soon at home I'll be,
  Be with Thee where Thou art.

October 16, 1860.

A REFLECTION.

THE Autumn leaves are falling fast,
Presaging Winter's stormy blast;
Denuded are the shady trees
By the cold north-eastern breeze.

All faded are the flow'rets fair
That decked but now our gay parterre;
Gone is their fragrance, gone their grace,
Run is their short but lovely race.

How chill and withering is the wind,
Bringing the lone churchyard to mind,
Filling the heart with sad dismay
To see all Nature thus decay.

'Tis so with man—he droops and dies,
And in the silent grave he lies,
Till dawn shall bright eternal spring,
When Heaven and earth with joy shall sing.

October 21, 1860.

COMMUNION HYMN.

EET me, oh! my heavenly Father,
  On this great festal day,
And on the high, the holy mount,
  Thy grace and love display.

Meet me, oh! my loving Father,
  As I draw nigh to Thee,
I come through Him who is the way,
  And who hath died for me.

Meet me, oh! my precious Saviour,
  Oh! hear me as I pray,
And in the fountain of Thy blood
  Wash all my sins away.

Meet me at Thy holy table,
  And show Thyself to me,
Oh! make mine heart within to burn
  With holy love to Thee.

Meet me, oh! Thou Holy Spirit,
  And waft my soul above,
To join the harpings round the throne,
  And hymn redeeming love.

Meet, meet, me as I swell the song,
That angel song of praise,
Aid me as Jesus' love I sing
In sweet seraphic lays

October 28, 1860.

TO A YOUNG FRIEND.

M AY many joyous years be thine,
A nd may thy path be bright,
R ejoice thou in the Lord alway,
G lad e'en in darkest night;
A mid this scene of care and strife
R epose on Jesus' love,
E re long thou shalt attain in peace
T hy happy home above.

H appy and peaceful mayst thou be
U pon thy natal day,
S unny and calm may thy path be
B right, bright thy pilgrim way;
A nd as thou tread'st this vale of tears,
N e'er may tears dim thine eye,
D ark clouds ne'er dim thy sky;

M uch good mayst thou be spared to do,
A nd ever happy be,
C onfide in Jesus, who hath said,
" R est and abide in Me;
I n storm or calm, in sun or shade,
T rust ever in My love."
C ast, then, on Him thine ev'ry care,
H e will thy Portion prove,
I n life, in death, He 'll be with thee,
E 'en till thou rest above.

November 5, 1860.

THE FALLEN LEAF.

NE lovely, calm, bright summer's eve
  I wandered forth alone,
And seated me in a lone spot,
  On an old moss-grown stone.

Alone with Jesus there I sat,
  Enwrapt in holy thought,
Enjoying commune near with Him,
  All earthly things forgot.

Of Heaven's joys my soul was lost
  In contemplation sweet,
When, suddenly, a withered leaf
  Fell trembling at my feet.

Silent I gazed, as there it lay,
  Reft from its parent tree ;
And as I gazed, methought it seemed
  A warning sent to me.

With angel voice it seemed to say,
  " Thus shalt thou fade and die,
For thou mayst droop ere this year close,
  Yea, in the grave may lie."

Then did I close mine eyes, and raise
  Mine heart to God in prayer,
That for the solemn hour of death
  He would my soul prepare.

Nor was this vision given once
  When I was thus alone,
But thrice, when on the wings of prayer
  Soared had I to God's throne.

Each warning, then, may I improve,
  And watch, and wait, and pray,
That for the messenger of peace
  I ready be alway.

For ah ! like to that leaflet sere,
  Laid low I soon may be ;
May Jesus' arms then welcome me,
  For to His breast I 'll flee.

November 7, 1860.

ACROSTIC.

TO JEANIE.

OYOUS and happy be this day,
A nd may love gild thy pilgrim way,
N e'er daunted be, but onward haste,
E ach golden moment do not waste.

C ome, come anew to God this day,
U pon Him rest, He is thy Stay ;
N ought from His heart shall e'er thee sever,
N one from His hand shall pluck thee ever.
I n Him aye trust, He cares for thee,
N o night of gloom shalt thou e'er see,
G o on thy way, lean on His arm,
H e shall protect thee from all harm,
A nd when life's pilgrimage is o'er,
M ay He thee hail on yonder shore.

November 8, 1860.

"NOT LOST, BUT GONE BEFORE."

THIS sad, sad day, has dawned again,
    Which fills thine heart with sorrow,
But oh ! may Jesus point thy soul
    To Heaven's bright to-morrow.

When re-united to that friend,
    Nought, nought shall e'er thee sever,
Together ye shall dwell in love
    For ever and for ever.

For ah ! in that bright, better land
    No tender ties are broken,
For there the mournful word, Farewell,
    Shall nevermore be spoken.

Ten years have o'er thee slowly rolled
    Since she from thee was riven,
But oh ! rejoice that thy loved one
    Reigns now a saint in Heaven.

She waits thee there, soon shall ye meet
    Before the throne of glory,
And through Heaven's bright, eternal day,
    Recount life's finished story.

'Neath Jesus' loving smile ye'll rest
  In amaranthine bowers;
Ye'll follow Him 'mong pastures green
  And never-fading flowers.

Then, cheer thee, cheer thee, mourning one,
  The time is short and fleeting;
Life's feverish dream will soon be o'er,
  And then thy happy meeting.

Yet patient wait, and cheerful be,
  'Though life be ofttimes dreary,
For walking closely with thy God,
  Ne'er, ne'er shalt thou feel weary.

God's time is best, then onward haste,
  Though faint, be yet pursuing,
The night of death swift speedeth on,
  Oh, then, be up and doing.

And does this thought not solace thee,
  That she can sorrow never?
Is done with trials, cares, and toils,
  Nor sins, nor suffers ever!

She, with the glorious ransomed band,
  Her Saviour-God is praising,
And, with the holy angel throng,
  Is hallelujahs raising.

Then dry thy tears, the Bridegroom comes!
  Oh, be thy lamp bright burning!
The morn of glory draweth near,
  Watch, wait for His returning.

November 16, 1860.

ACROSTIC.

TO A FRIEND.

OYOUS and peaceful be this day;
E re thou resume thy pilgrim way,
S eek strength where it alone is found,
S o shall thy days with peace abound ;
I n light or shade, trust in the Lord,
E 'en 'mid dark gloom, cling to His word.

L ean on His gentle, loving arm,
U pon Him rest secure from harm,
K eep close to Him, He's alway nigh
E ach prayer to hear, to mark each sigh.

November 30, 1860.

ON THE GRAVEYARD.

GOD'S acre! oh, most blessed name
　　That to a graveyard's given,
For there the precious seed is sown
　　That blossom shall in Heaven.

Let this sweet thought us soothe and cheer,
　　When loved ones droop and die,
Though to the narrow tomb consigned,
　　Their spirits live on high.

As in that hallowed place we walk,
　　How precious is the thought,
That of the thousands mouldering there,
　　Not one shall be forgot.

For God doth guard the sleeping dust,
　　'Tis precious in His sight,
'Twill rest in undisturbed repose
　　Till dawn shall morning light.

Sabbatic silence reigns around,
　　Which makes our sad heart thrill,
E'en Nature wears an aspect grave,
　　All is so peaceful, still.

And as we bend o'er yon lone graves,
 We may, though weeping, hear
The voices of departed ones
 Fall, soothing, on our ear.

" Weep not for us, we weep not now,
 With sorrow we have done,
We now are happier far than you,
 The crown of life is won.

" Then dry your tears and hasten on,
 Soon shall ye reach the goal,
And in the bright, the better land,
 Shall rest your happy soul.

" What we now are ye soon shall be,
 From sin, from sorrow free,
Ye 'll rest in Jesus' deathless love,
 And all His glory see.

" No death can e'er invade our home,
 All there is endless joy,
Pure, perfect bliss shall soon be yours,
 Full, free, without alloy ! "

Thus cheered, we quit that sacred spot,
 To speed us on our way,
In the fond hope that soon 'twill end
 In Heaven's eternal day.

December 1, 1860.

ACROSTIC.

TO A FRIEND.

 A Y many happy years be thine,
A nd may love on thy pathway shine ;
R est in the Lord, He cares for thee,
Y ea, He thy Strength and Song will be.

S mooth be thine upward, onward way,
M ay Jesus bless thee day by day,
I n storm or calm bask 'neath His smile,
T rust in the Lord, He 'll care beguile,
H e 'll guide thee through life's little while.

December 6, 1860.

A FATHER TO HIS INFANT DAUGHTER.

LOW'RET of promise, bud of Spring,
I love to watch thee blossoming,
Thy sunny brow, thy radiant smile,
Do all the cares of life beguile.

Thy rosy cheeks, thy sparkling eyes,
Show that thou know'st not tears nor sighs,
All's now with thee a time of joy,
As yet no cares can thee annoy.

Ah! lovely bud, no one doth know
What yet may be thy path below,
Whether thy sky be tranquil, bright,
Or clouded o'er by sorrow's night.

Oh! mayst thou go in early youth
To Him who is "The Life, the Truth,"
He will thee love, thee keep, thee bless,
He will be all thy Righteousness.

Then may'st thou give to Him life's morn,
The little lambs He does not scorn,
But bids them to His bosom come,
Their happy, their eternal home.

In slumber soft I see thee rest,
Close prest to thy fond mother's breast,
Who bends on thee an anxious eye,
Whilst falls a tear so silently.

And as thou calmly sleepest there,
For thee she breathes the earnest prayer
That thou, upon the Saviour's breast,
Mayst through life's day as peaceful rest.

Thou smilest, sweet one, can it be
That angels whisper soft to thee,
And bid thee leave this world of ours,
To bloom in amaranthine bowers.

It may be so ; thou soon, fair gem,
May deck thy Saviour's diadem,
Through endless ages thou wilt shine,
A trophy bright of love divine.

Yet ah ! I fain would keep thee here,
My heart with thy glad smile to cheer,
And as thou dost advance in years,
Ne'er be thy bright eye dimmed with tears.

Yet grief will have its dreary day,
But if Christ Jesus sun thy way,
Serene and happy thou wilt be,
Till crowned with immortality.

He will thy dawning day defend,
And be through life thy constant Friend,
Until we meet in Heaven above,
To share His deep, eternal love !

December 10, 1860.

ACROSTIC.

TO A FRIEND.

E VER may'st thou happy be,
L ive to God, He loveth thee,
I n the shade, trust thou His love,
Z ealous be time to improve;
A s thou tread'st this vale of tears,
B anish gloomy doubts and fears,
E ver lean on Jesus' breast,
T rust in Him, He 'll give thee rest,
H e will make thee happy, blest.

E 'en now tranquil may'st thou be,
L ove shall gild each cloud to thee,
D aily, life shall be more bright,
E ver walking in His sight,
R adiant aye shall be thy light.

M any sunny years be thine,
A lway hear the voice divine,
" C ome, my child, anew to Me,
R est and peace I give to thee,
I am thine, and thou art Mine,
T rust thou in My love divine."
C heered thus on thy pilgrim way,
H e shall bless thee day by day,
I n His strength, then, onward go,
E ver haste from all below.

December 13, 1860.

ON PATIENCE.

GOD give me grace and strength to bear the
  little ills of life,
And may I patient be, amid this scene of
  ceaseless strife.

My little crosses, O may I with patience aye endure,
There is a needs-be for them all, they make the soul
  more pure.

" Let patience have her perfect work," exert her gentle
  sway,
For many are the thorns and briars that spring up day
  by day.

Fain would they check mine onward course, and lead
  my feet astray,
But still I hear a voice of love, " This is the narrow way."

The lighter sorrows of this life are ofttimes hard to bear,
More hard than heavy chastisements, but I will not
  despair.

I will not pine when others joy, I 'll patient, silent be,
Cold is the world, its frown I 'll face, if God but smile
  on me.

Undaunted by its bitter scoff, I 'll give myself to prayer,
God will me hear and strengthen me, patient its taunts
  to bear.

In His strength I can all things do, can meekly suffer
  wrong;
E'en while the world me slight and scorn, in *Him* I
  shall be strong.

Cold looks, harsh words, oft wound my heart, friends
  false and heartless prove,
But I will turn from them to God, and glory in *His*
  love.

Bridged o'er is each deep rolling flood, rainbowed the
  darkest skies,
Each cloud a silver lining has, which Faith alone descries.

All the daily, little crosses, I meet with in my way,
Like Jesus, may I patient bear, nor from them turn away.

Then pleasantly shall life glide on, a gladsome, summer
  day,
No clouds of storm, no shades of night, shall fill me
  with dismay.

For why? my heart in Heaven, this earth with lightsome
  foot I 'll tread,
And on my Father's bosom rest my weary, aching head.

My soul in patience I 'll possess, ne'er shall I fretful be,
I 'll meekly bear and do His will, for He sustaineth me.

To bear and forbear, oh, be this my heart's wish and
    delight,
With gentle words and loving looks may I all ill
    requite.

O may I to God's glory live, a bright ensample be,
Of meekness, patience, gentleness, of deep humility.

December 23, 1860.

ON CHRISTMAS DAY.

 LL hail the holy, gladsome morn
That saw the Lord of Glory born!
Let it be kept a holiday,
To cheer the pilgrim on his way.

In lordly hall, in lowly cot,
Ne'er be this holy day forgot,
Be it a day of chastened mirth,
That calls to mind the Saviour's birth.

That Day of days, deep fraught with love,
That Day which from the heavens above
Was heralded by angel voice,
Commanding all men to rejoice.

For Christ a child of days became,
" Emmanuel," how sweet a name!
The same when in the manger laid
As when the heavens and earth He made.

Bethlehem's babe, yet mighty God,
Sinless, alone, this earth He trod,
Endured life's sorrows, pangs, and shame,
That we might triumph in His name.

For us He suffered, groaned, and died,
Lord over all, the Crucified !
And now in Him we stand complete,
And are for Heaven's glories meet.

And as we share the festal cheer
With Christian friends in Jesus dear,
Let love with friendship be combined,
As mistletoe with holly's twined.

Sweet evergreens ! ye know no change,
Our thoughts would take a higher range,
Think of *His* love, 'tis evergreen,
Brightest aye in saddest scene.

Yet sorrow mingles with our joy,
There is no gold without alloy,
For ah ! as wanes the circling year,
How may a loved one's missing here !

No board but there's the vacant seat
Of one whom we were wont to meet,
The lovely form, the smiling face,
Are claspt in death's chill, cold embrace

May not their spirits present be,
Communing with us peacefully,
Inviting us to soar away
To glory's bright, unending day.

Ere circles round another year,
Our chair *too* may be empty here,
Yet hail, auspicious holy morn
That saw the Lord of Glory born !

December 25, 1860.

ACROSTIC.

NEW YEAR'S HYMN.

LET ev'ry soul with gratitude be filled this festal
day,
I n ev'ry heart let joy abound, that on the
Lord doth stay,
F or He on whom our hopes depend will bless this
new-born year,
E nabling us from day to day to spend it in His fear.

I n sun or shade, we 'll trust His love, and on His
bosom rest,
S o shall our path be tranquil, smooth, though by
afflictions prest.

B eneath the shadow of His wings He will us alway
hide,
U pon us is His watchful eye, He 's ever at our side,
T o whisper, "Fear not, oh! my child, thy loving
Father's nigh,

A mid the changing scenes of life upon My love rely."

F leet as an arrow from the bow do days and years
  steal on,
L ife's little tale will soon be told, life's pilgrimage be done,
E 'en now a streak of morning dawns, the night will
  soon be o'er,
E re long eternal day will break on yonder radiant shore;
T ime, on untiring wing, speeds on, nought can its
  course impede,
I ts golden hours who can recall ? then let us *now*
  take heed,
N *ow* let us fight the fight of faith, and onward urge
  our way,
G od will us bless and give us strength according to
  our day.

D ream we may not of to-morrow, though sunny be
  to-day,
A nd though Hope on our pathway strew her many
  flow'rets gay,
Y et, ere the morrow dawn, they may have faded all away.

S weet, oh, *how* sweet ! to see the bow when darkness
  shrouds the sky,
W hen life's fond, cherished hopes decay, when loved
  ones fade and die,
I f in Christ Jesus, all is well, they've reached their
  home on high ;
F ade, too, shall we, it may be soon, e'en ere this New
  Year close,
T hen let us be preparèd for our last, our long repose ;
L ife's little day will soon be o'er, its hours are fleeting
  fast,
Y ear after year glides swiftly on, Time will not alway last.

W ith hearts devoted to our God, we'll work, and
watch, and pray,

I n everything His Glory seek, and serve Him day by
day;

L ife, then, will be all sunny, bright, for He will on
us smile,

L ove, Faith, and Hope shall gild our path through
all our little while.

I n cloudy days, as in the bright, we'll list His gentle
voice,

"T rust in My changeless, deathless love, and in Me
aye rejoice."

eace, Mine own peace, I give to thee, from guilt,
from sin, thee free,

A ll through the darksome vale of years I ever will
keep thee;

S peed on thy way, strong in My strength, lean on My
loving arm,

S hrink not when foes around thee throng, I'll keep
thee safe from harm."

A h! thus cheered on, ere long we'll reach Emmanuel's
happy land,

W here, with the crown of glory wreathed, before
God's throne we'll stand,

A nd, clad in robes of radiant light, we'll sin, we'll
sorrow never!

Y ea, we shall live and reign with Him for ever and
for ever!

January 1, 1861.

NEW YEAR'S HYMN FOR CHILDREN

ARK! another year is past,
Life's brief day is fleeting fast ;
But it will not too soon end,
If Thou, Jesus, be our *Friend*.

Soon youth's pleasures pass away,
Soon earth's fondest hopes decay ;
But life's day will all be bright,
If Thou, Jesus, be our *Light*.

Prone are we to err and stray,
Prone to leave the narrow way ;
But our footsteps ne'er shall slide,
If Thou, Jesus, be our *Guide*.

Swift life's brightest joys may end,
Swift the shades of night descend ;
But no griefs can us annoy,
If Thou, Jesus, be our *Joy*.

Cherish'd friends may fade and die,
Loved ones in the grave may lie ;
But we 'll faint not in the strife,
If Thou, Jesus, be our *Life*.

Oft our life is but begun,
When 'tis said, " Thy race is run ;"
But we'll be for ever blest,
If Thou, Jesus, be our *Rest*.

January, 1, 1861.

ANOTHER NEW YEAR'S HYMN FOR
CHILDREN.

 NOTHER year has passed away
Since last we hailed a New-Year's day,
The stream of life glides swiftly on,
Soon will its rapid course be run.

Life's little day is fleeting fast,
This new-born year may be our last,
For since we saw last New-Year's day,
How many a friend has passed away!

Ere this New Year its race has run,
Our life's short journey may be done,
We, too, may fade, and droop, and die,
And in the silent grave may lie.

Then hear us, Jesus, as we pray,
That Thou wouldst bless us day by day;
Us cleanse anew from guilt and sin,
As we another year begin.

Oh! listen to our song of praise,
Which we, from grateful hearts, now raise;
We thank Thee for Thy mercies past,
And future cares on Thee we cast.

I

Lord Jesus, may we grow in grace,
Until we rest in Thine embrace,
Where, from all sin and sorrow free,
Our souls shall find their all in Thee.

January 1, 1861.

ON THE DEATH OF A SISTER.

WEET sister mine,
Rest now is thine,
Thine earthly cares are o'er ;
Dried are thy tears,
Gone are thy fears,
Thou'rt safe on yonder shore.

Run is thy race,
In death's embrace
I see thee lying there ;
Yet 'tis not thee,
Whom now I see,
'Tis but the casket fair.

The jewel's gone,
Up it has flown
The Saviour's crown to gem ;
Ah ! radiant, bright,
In Heaven's light
Is that fair diadem.

Thou sleepest now,
Calm is thy brow
In death, as 'twas in life ;
Thy gladsome smile
Did cares beguile,
Didst banish envy, strife.

Thy merry voice
Made all rejoice,
Thou wast so full of mirth ;
A sunbeam thou,
Thy placid brow
Made glad thy home and hearth.

We, sisters, gaze,
In sad amaze,
To see what death has done ;
The form is dead,
The spirit's fled,
To Jesus' bosom gone.

Cut down at noon,
Yet not too soon,
Thy day of mourning's o'er ;
Thy short career
Of suffering here
Is ended evermore.

Thrice blessèd now,
Wreathed is thy brow,
The fadeless palm is thine ;
Thy sparkling eye
Now beams on high
With love and joy divine.

Thy children dear
Will mourn thee here,
Will miss thy gentle love ;
Orphans are they,
But through life's day
God will a parent prove.

To Heaven's bright sphere
Thy partner dear,
Soared but two months ago ;
Now thou art gone,
Too swiftly flown,
But God hath willed it so.

He beckoned thee
From earth to flee,
Ye were not severed long ,
In robes of white,
All dazzling bright,
Ye hymn the sweet new song.

Ye walk in light,
There falls no night
On yonder tranquil shore,
There shall ye rest
On Jesus' breast,
" Not lost, but gone before."

A few short years
Of sighs and tears,
We'll meet for evermore ;
Together there,
Heaven's bliss we'll share,
And part, ah ! nevermore !

January 5, 1861.

TO LIZZIE.

HOW shall I now address you,
  My little Lizzie dear,
As you this day in health and strength
  Begin another year?

You ask me not to lecture you,
  That you will read it not,
Then what to say, my own dear child,
  Costs me some little thought.

May thy life be all sunny, bright,
  A gladsome summer day,
May radiant hope bestrew thy path
  With flow'rets sweet and gay.

But should a cloudlet gloom thy sky,
  Soon will it pass away,
For thou a beauteous sunbeam art
  To cheer life's lonesome day.

A rosebud in this wilderness
  To gladden us art thou,
Thy sparkling eye with mirth doth shine,
  Aye sunny is thy brow.

I love to see thee meek and mild
  As lily of the vale,
Modest as is the violet sweet
  That decks the shady dale.

For as that lowly floweret
  Loves in the shade to bloom,
Diffusing through the balmy air
  A fragrant, sweet perfume.

So mayest thou, my little one,
  Blessings around thee shower,
That thy loved presence may be felt
  Like that sweet, modest flower.

Thus loving and being loved by all,
  Thou'lt useful, cheerful be ;
Year after year shall swift glide on,
  Yet bright they'll be to thee.

Brighter and brighter be thy day,
  Till fall the shades of even,
And then may Jesus welcome thee
  To all the joys of Heaven.

Be many happy birthdays thine,
  May sunshine round thee play,
Is thy fond mother's earnest wish,
  On this, thy natal day.

And now, " adieu," mine own loved one,
  Say not I've lectured thee,
To see thee good is all my prayer,
  Then happy wilt thou be.

January 13, 1861.

ACROSTIC.

L IFE to thee is just begun,
    I s a race still yet to run,
    Z ealous be to run it well,
    Z ealous others to excel ;
I n thine onward bright career,
E ver haste, and banish fear.

S unshine doth around thee play,
A ll 's with thee a summer day,
W hen no clouds bedim thy sky,
E ver sparkling is thine eye,
R adiant, sunny, full of glee,
S uch may life be aye to thee.

M ayst thou ever happy be,
I n life's morn from sorrow free,
T ime may bring its darksome night,
C alm then wait for morning's light,
H e that doeth all things well,
E 'en will darkest clouds dispel ;
L ife again will be all bright,
L ove shall gild its darkest night.

January 13, 1861.

RESIGNATION.

HUSHED be each rising, murmuring thought,
　　Oh, ne'er would I repine,
But joy, when in the furnace cast,
　　Which would my soul refine,
Which would the dross all purge away,
　　And make my graces shine.

From Thine own hand the bitter cup
　　I'll take most cheerfully,
'Tis mingled by a Father's love,
　　Who careth still for me,
Then drink it to the dregs I will,
　　Whate'er the mixture be.

Oh! give me grace to kiss the rod,
　　When healthful days are gone.
'Tis Christ-like to endure, to say,
　　" Father, Thy will be done,
Thou knowest what is best for me,
　　Thy will and mine be one."

When hearts grow cold, to Thee alone
　　I'll turn for sympathy,
For Thou hast felt its want, oh! then
　　I'll to Thy bosom flee,
And weep the bitter, burning tears
　　Of heart-felt agony.

When grief and anguish wring my heart,
  When sorrow clouds my brow,
When heavy is my cross to bear,
  My Strength, my Joy art Thou,
Then to Thy will, howe'er severe,
  I cheerfully will bow.

When pining sickness wastes my frame,
  When I am sore opprest,
I'll in Thy hands calm, passive lie,
  Like babe on mother's breast,
Yea, I will ever patient be,
  For Thou wilt give me rest.

January 21, 1861.

EMMAUS.

 "ABIDE with me," O precious Saviour !
    In sorrow's darksome night,
When skies are shrouded with a pall,
    Be Thou a shining light.

"Lo, I am with thee !" mourning soul,
    When starless is thy night,
My promises shall cheer thy soul,
    And make thy sky all bright.

"Abide with me," O loving Jesus !
    Through all life's lonesome way,
Do Thou its weariness beguile,
    Be Thou my Sun, my Stay.

"Lo, I am with thee !" lonely one,
    When thy loved ones are gone,
My near-felt presence shall thee cheer,
    E'en till life's journey's done.

"Abide with me," O gracious Saviour !
    When life's a gladsome day,
Oh, make mine heart with love to burn,
    And guide me lest I stray.

" Lo, I am with thee !" prosp'rous soul,
  When sunshine gilds thy way,
I 'll thee preserve from all the snares,
  That would thee lead astray.

" Abide with me," O gentle Jesus !
  When fall the shades of night,
Do Thou illume the valley gloom,
  Make Thou its darkness, light.

" Lo, I am with thee !" sorrowing one,
  To soothe thy weeping heart,
Thy bleeding wounds I will bind up,
  Will healing balm impart.

" Abide with me," O holy Saviour !
  At morning, noon, and night,
Refresh my soul with heav'nly grace,
  Me fill with calm delight.

" Lo, I am with thee !" prayerful soul,
  To list thy gentle sigh,
The silent breathings of thy soul
  Shall e'en to Me come nigh.

" Abide with me," O lowly Jesus !
  When on a bed of death
I 'll lay me in Thine arms of love,
  And gently yield my breath.

" Lo, I am with thee !" suff'ring one,
  When sore by pain opprest,
Thy weary, throbbing head shall be
  Calm pillowed on My breast.

" Abide with me," O faithful Saviour !
 When friends around me weep,
As laid upon that bed of pain,
 In Thee I fall asleep.

'' Lo, I am with thee !" dying one,
 I 'll clasp thee in Mine arms,
Thou 'lt safely pass through Jordan's waves,
 Free from all death's alarms.

" Abide with me," O blessed Jesus !
 Through Heaven's eternal day,
Then shall I see Thee as Thou art,
 And praise Thy name for aye.

'' Lo, I am with thee !" ransomed saint,
 When safe on yonder shore,
Thou shalt My crown and glory share,
 Be with Me evermore !

January 27, 1861.

SUMMER FRIENDS.

F summer friends beware,
Heartless and false are they,
They us caress and court,
When life is bright and gay ;
When skies are cloudless and serene,
These friends around our path are seen.

Whilst roses round us bloom,
How lavish are their smiles !
Whilst sunshine round us plays,
How treacherous their wiles !
Then trust them not, or soon ye 'll find
The briar with the rose entwined.

Let but the sky grow dark,
Let but the black clouds scowl,
Let but the storm arise,
Let but the tempest howl,
Let lightnings flash and thunders roar,
Such friends are gone for evermore.

I would not call them friends,
Not worthy such a name,
To no respect or love
Can they at all lay claim,
Who in cold winter's stormy day
Can leave us to its rage a prey.

They're like the butterflies
Which sport in summer sun,
Let but a show'ret fall,
These insects bright are gone;
Thus summer friends, like butterflies,
All flee whene'er the tempests rise.

They heed us not, nor care
That we should weep alone,
They pass us coldly by,
As if unseen, unknown;
Then, faithless, heartless, false are they,
Who shun us in the darksome day.

February 10, 1861.

WINTER FRIENDS.

RECIOUS are winter friends,
'Their friendship never ends,
In sunshine or in darkest shade,
Their love, deep, full, and free,
Is like the myrtle-tree,
An evergreen, which ne'er shall fade.

As the green holly-tree,
Which we in winter see,
With berries red, fadeless and gay,
Cheers us amid the gloom,
Which dark is as the tomb,
Such are these friends in sorrow's day.

When fond hopes are blighted,
When we are benighted,
When darkness o'ershadows our skies,
Then those loved ones are near,
Us to solace and cheer,
In our sorrow to sympathise.

When summer friends grow cold,
Their arms will us enfold,
And clasp us more close than before;
Ne'er, ne'er will they leave us,
Nor will they deceive us,
But to us they will cling evermore.

Not like our summer friends,
Whose love with sunlight ends,
Who flee whene'er night's shadows fall ;
Nor like the butterfly,
Who will take wing and fly,
When the sky is clad o'er with a pall.

Faithful, true, and sincere,
To our hearts justly dear,
Are those winter friends who so us love ;
Worthy the name of friend,
Their love can know no end,
It blooms here but to ripen above.

February 18, 1861.

PRAYER.

" **ESUS!** *be not far from me,*"
E ver shall I trust in Thee,
S ave and keep me evermore,
U ntil safe on yonder shore,
S torms shall feared be nevermore!

B e Thou o'er life's troubled sea,
E ver Pilot unto me.

N ot afraid of roughest tide,
O nward may my bark swift glide,
T ill safe moored on yonder side.

F ar from port I yet may be,
A ngry waves may pass o'er me,
R est I calmly shall in Thee.

F rom all fear Thou wilt keep me,
R age then may life's stormy sea,
O 'er it with Thee as my Guide,
M ay my bark aye safely glide.

M e preserve, whate'er betide,
E ver 'neath Thy wing me hide.

PROMISE.

" T is I, be not afraid,"
T rust thou in My gracious aid.

I s thy bark 'mid billows tost ?
S tay on Me, 'twill ne'er be lost.

I am nigh when seas run high.

B e thy pillow My fond breast,
E 'en 'mid storms thou 'lt peaceful rest.

N ot alone when skies are bright,
O h ! no, e'en in gloomiest night
T empests ne'er shall thee affright.

A fraid, then, thou may'st never be,
F loat thy bark shall o'er life's sea,
R aging waves may round thee rise,
A nd though black may be thy skies,
I am near in that dark hour,
D oubt not then My love and power.

February 28, 1861.

BIRTHDAY REFLECTIONS.

NOTHER year of suffering hath slowly
  sped away,
And I am spared again to see another
  natal day.

Ah ! I cannot call it "happy," 'tis not so *now* to me,
For healthful days and gladsome scenes can ne'er recallèd be.

Yet memory brings them back to mind on this sad
  mournful day,
Such deeply sad rememberings can never pass away.

Year after year they rise to view more vivid than the last,
But yet I would not them forget, I would retrace the past.

They tell me that my God is good and faithful unto me,
But for restraining grace and love what might I not
  now be ?

Hath He not led me all my way e'en to this present day,
And now He will not me forsake, but will me keep alway.

Thus cheered and nerved I would anew give heart and
  soul to God,
Devote mine ev'ry power to Him, nor fear the chastening
  rod.

It tells me of a Father's love, who chastens to refine,
That when His children He rebukes, 'tis needed discipline.

Then shall I meekly bear my cross, how hard soe'er
    it be,
For ah! it is not like to that which Jesus bore for
    me.

In close communion with my God I'll tread this lone-
    some vale,
And, leaning on my Saviour's arm, my strength can never
    fail.

For earnest prayer doth nerve my heart, me fits for toils
    and strife,
Keeps me aye cheerful, hopeful, calm, amid the storms
    of life.

" Father, my little ones be Thine," is still my constant
    prayer,
Oh, may we meet in Heaven at last, and Jesus' glory
    share.

A grateful heart is mine this day, for kind my Father's
    been,
Throughout the year now past and gone His hand in all
    I've seen.

Oh, may I in His presence spend my life's short, fleeting
    day,
And by my pen advance His cause, His grace, His love
    display.

My feeble efforts may He bless to touch the sinner's
heart,
To heal the wounded bleeding soul, and heavenly balm
impart.

Year after year doth pass away, ere long my last will
come,
Oh, then may I preparèd be to go with Jesus home.

March 19, 1861.

THE RESURRECTION.

OON will the night of time be o'er,
  The morn of joy draws near !
That morn before whose dazzling light
  Night's shades will disappear :
When the last awful trumpet peals,
  Eternal day will break,
The living then shall changèd be,
  The sleeping dead shall wake.

Each shrouded form shall hear its sound,
  And leave its lonesome bed,
On that dread morn when Jesus comes
  To judge the quick and dead :
All shall come forth to meet their Judge,
  Where'er their graves may be,
Whether they sleep in churchyards still,
  Or in the blue lone sea.

The holy dead shall first arise,
  To bloom in endless day,
Amid the bowers of Paradise,
  Ne'ermore to fade away :
They'll flourish near the Tree of Life,
  Beneath its branches rest,
They'll follow where the Lamb shall lead,
  Redeemèd, holy, blest.

On harps of gold, as ages roll,
  They'll hymn His matchless love ;
They'll serve the Lord who brought them safe
  To that bright land above :
There shall they meet to part no more
  From loved ones gone before,
No tender ties can broken be
  On that celestial shore !

Yet, ah ! what separations sad
  Shall on that morn take place ;
For have not some rejected Christ—
  Despised His offered grace ?
These, by their Sovereign Judge consigned
  To everlasting pains,
Shall have their portion in that place
  Where night eternal reigns.

Mother from child, husband from wife,
  Friend torn from friend may be,
Who this tear-watered valley trod
  In closest company :
Then let us see that we are one
  In Christ with those we love,
That on that morn we all may rise,
  And soar to bliss above.

Then shall we meet the Lord in peace,
  Be of that glorious band,
Who'll sing around the throne of God
  The songs of that bright land.

Soon dawn shall that calm, cloudless day,
  On which shall fall no night,
No clouds shall flit athwart that sky—
  God's smile is Heaven's light.

Ah ! who can paint the glories of
  That Resurrection morn ?
Or who conceive the holiness
  That shall our souls adorn ?
For, clad in Jesus' snow-white robe,
  Like Him we 'll holy be,
Then ah ! how bright, how calm shall be
  The Sabbath of Eternity !

April 5, 1861.

K

ACROSTIC.

TO A YOUNG FRIEND.

J OYOUS and happy be this day,
A nd may hope cheer thine onward way,
N ow, if thou bask 'neath love divine,
E ach day shall brighter, brighter shine.

D escend may ofttimes shades of night,
I t cannot, will not, aye be light,
C ome will the darksome, cloudy sky,
K eep then to Jesus very nigh,
S ecure in Him thou 'lt storms defy :
O n Him repose, trust in Him ever !
N ought from His heart shall e'er thee sever !

G ive, then, to God thy youthful Spring,
R ich beauty may thy Summer bring,
A utumn with fruits shall laden be,
N o darksome Winter shalt thou see,
T hy life shall pass so cheerfully.

April 13, 1861.

TO TOM.

HIS happy day has dawned again,
   And what shall I now say,
Thy mother's wishes best are thine
   On this, thy natal day.

Thou hast life's duties now begun,
   O mayst thou prosp'rous be,
O may thy path be strewed with flowers,
   May fortune smile on thee.

Much good mayst thou be spared to do,
   A blessing be to all,
A comfort to thy loving friends
   When darksome days shall fall.

Beware the snares around thee set,
   To lead thy soul astray,
Resist temptation in God's strength,
   Oh ! keep the narrow way.

Oh ! choose in this, thy gladsome Spring,
   The good, the better part ;
Oh ! give to God thy life's fresh morn,
   Him love with all thine heart.

Then beauteous shall thy Summer be,
  In holiness arrayed ;
Thy life shall aye be cheerful, calm,
  In sunshine as in shade.

Thine Autumn, too, shall fruitful be,
  With holy deeds replete ;
Life's stream shall tranquil, smoothly glide,
  Till thou for Heaven art meet.

So that, when dreary Winter comes,
  'Twill not be so to thee,
For, looking back on days well spent,
  Thou shalt calm, happy be.

And when the heavenly race is run,
  The victor's crown be thine,
And in the Christian's home above,
  Bask thou 'neath love divine.

There may we meet, life's trials o'er,
  And be for ever blest,
With Jesus and our dear loved ones
  Enjoy eternal rest.

And now, adieu, mine own dear boy,.
  The Lord thee bless this day,
Cause shine on thee His gracious face,
  Now ! henceforth ! and for aye !

April 17, 1861.

TO ELIZABETH.

LL hail ! Christian pilgrim,
 On this happy day ;
Since last I addressed thee
 A year's pass'd away.
How swiftly time glides,
 Then linger, ah ! never ;
" Upward and onward,"
 Thy motto be ever !

Serve the Lord, pilgrim,
 Him love more and more ;
Follow Him gladly,
 His goodness adore :
Heart and soul give to God,
 Devoted be ever !
Live to Him wholly,
 Deny Him, ah ! never !

In happy days, pilgrim,
 Walk humbly with God,
When all is bright sunshine,
 Oh ! bless thou the Lord :
Be thankful, be faithful,
 Forget thy God never !
Cling to Him closely,
 Praise the Lord, ever !

In sorrow's night, pilgrim,
  Thy God will be near,
To strengthen and soothe thee,
  Thy sad heart to cheer :
Then kiss the rod meekly,
  Oh ! faint not, nor fear,
A Father's hand wields it,
  To whom thou art dear.

Should tempests rage, pilgrim,
  Should clouds storm thy sky,
O ! look unto Jesus,
  On *His* love rely :
The storm He will calm,
  Then trust in Him, ever !
The port thou wilt reach
  Where tempests rise never !

Then onward, haste, pilgrim,
  Press homeward to God,
Ah ! fear not to tread
  Life's rough, thorny road ;
Soon, soon it will lead thee
  To Canaan's fair shore,
Where sin and where sorrow
  Shall vex thee no more !

April 26, 1861.

TO A YOUNG FRIEND ON LEAVING HOME.

 BOUT to leave thy home, Willie !
    To cross the pathless deep,
Around thee be God's arms of love,
    May He thee safely keep.

Adieu thou 'lt bid to friends, Willie !
    To tread an alien shore,
But may they aye in memory live,
    E'en till life's journey 's o'er.

'Twill cost thine heart a pang, Willie !
    To leave thy native land,
But if thy father's God be thine,
    He 'll lead thee by the hand.

Remember that His eye, Willie !
    Is ever bent on thee,
That if thou wilt but trust in Him,
    Thy faithful Friend He 'll be.

May prosperous days be thine, Willie !
    May fortune on thee smile,
And may love's banner o'er thee wave,
    Through all life's little while.

If diligent thou be, Willie !
  God will thy labours bless,
And if thou Him but love and serve,
  He 'll crown them with success.

And may the pleasant thought, Willie !
  That loved ones far away
Are thinking of thee day by day,
  Oft cheer thee on thy way.

Ah ! there 's a cherish'd spot, Willie !
  Where sever'd friends may meet,
And bear each other on their hearts—
  It is the Mercy-seat.

Revisit oft in thought, Willie !
  Thine own belovèd home,
But ah ! forget not that e'en there
  Sad changes soon may come.

Think too of No. 8, Willie !
  As well as No. 4,
For we 'll be speaking oft of thee,
  On yonder foreign shore.

Yes ! Time will tell on all, Willie !
  The circle thou dost leave,
Can not for aye remain the same,
  Yet I 'd not have thee grieve.

Death may invade thy home, Willie !
  But think of Heaven above,
And strive to meet thy loved ones there,
  A family of love. .

A family in the Lord, Willie !
  Must alway happy be,
In sun or shade, in calm or storm,
  God's gracious hand they see.

And oh ! may'st thou return, Willie !
  To thy dear native land,
And for many a happy year enjoy
  The labours of thine hand.

Blanks many there will be, Willie !
  Friends will have pass'd away,
But oh ! may this sweet thought be thine—
  We'll meet in Glory's Day.

I bid thee now "adieu," Willie !
  To God I thee commend,
May He thy Friend, thy Refuge prove,
  Until life's day shall end.

Then to the Christian's home, Willie !
  May'st thou admitted be,
And with thy God and loving friends
  Rejoice eternally.

My wishes best are thine, Willie !
  God speed thee on thy way,
And may we meet in Heaven at last,
  Secure in cloudless day.

May 1861.

TO MARY.

ANOTHER happy year, Mary!
  Hath swiftly sped away,
And with warmest heart-felt pleasure,
  I wish thee joy this day.

Bright, beauteous, gladsome be, Mary!
  Thy joyous summer-time,
Oh! be thy soul with grace adorned,
  E'en now in thy youth's prime.

Give God thy loving heart, Mary!
  And He thy Friend shall be,
Then shall thy bark glide peaceful on,
  E'en o'er life's stormiest sea.

Should e'er a lowering cloud, Mary!
  Bedim thy sunny sky,
To Jesus look, and in His love
  With confidence rely.

That day I'll ne'er forget, Mary!
  When thou to me wast given,
A beauteous rose-bud to be reared,
  For endless life, for Heaven.

Mingled were my feelings, Mary !
  As on my mournful breast
In innocence thou sleeping lay,
  In calm, seraphic rest ;

And as I gazed on thee, Mary !
  Hot tears bedimmed mine eye,
Unseen, unknown, save to my God
  Who then to me was nigh.

I thought upon the past, Mary !
  Sad it had been to me,
And I looked into the future,
  But light I could not see.

I locked thee in mine arms, Mary !
  Thee to my bosom prest,
Prayed God that thus thou might'st repose
  On Jesus' loving breast.

I gave thee then to God, Mary !
  Prayed Jesus thee to bless,
To be thy Shepherd and thy Friend,
  To be thy Righteousness.

And till this happy day, Mary !
  Hath God not faithful been ?
In all thy bygone, gladsome days,
  Hast thou His hand not seen ?

Then rest not in the race, Mary !
  Till at the goal thou stand,
And win the crown of amaranth
  From Jesus' gracious hand.

May roses round thee bloom, Mary !
   Thy life be calm, serene,
Ne'er may a cloudlet gloom thy sky,
   Without a rainbow seen.

May all things good be thine, Mary !
   May sunshine gild thy way,
Is thy fond Mother's earnest wish
   On this thy natal day.

June 1, 1861.

TO HELEN.

OW swiftly days and years glide on·!
E   'en as a dream they pass away,
L   ife! ah! 'tis but a race to run,
E   ach day press on, oh ! ne'er delay,
N   or tarry till the goal be won.

E   ach moment brings thee nearer home,
W   here dwell thy loved ones gone before ;
A   h ! they from Jesus ne'er shall roam,
R   est in His love they 'll evermore,
T   here's nought but joy on yonder shore.

S   ister ! may sunnier days be thine,
A   nd may light on thy pathway shine,
W   ith Jesus as thy faithful Friend,
E   'en darkest days in bliss shall end,
R   epose in Him, mistrust Him never !
S   o shall life's day be tranquil ever !

June 3, 1861.

PRAYER.

A S oft before a throne of grace
 We bend the knee in prayer,
As oft a God of mercy deigns
 To meet His children there ;
He listens to their feeblest cry,
 Their ev'ry whisper hears,
He marks their ev'ry groan and sigh,
 He counts their very tears.

The humble suppliant at the throne
 Is never turned away,
God will him hear, and strengthen him
 According to his day ;
The meek, the lowly contrite ones
 Are His peculiar care,
He bends on them a loving eye,
 He loves to hear their prayer.

He loves to cheer the drooping heart,
 To wipe away our tears,
To soothe our sorrows, heal our pains,
 And banish all our fears ;
On Him, then, we will cast our cares,
 To Him commit our way,
On Him roll all our guilt and sins,
 Our burdens day by day.

And as a child, confiding, leans
  Upon a mother's breast,
Assured that there it ever may
  In peace and safety rest;
So may we, Holy Father, be
  Close to Thy bosom prest,
And, circled by Thine arms of love,
  We'll tranquil be and blest.

And as that little one keeps close
  Unto his father's side,
Grasping his loving hand, that he
  May all his footsteps guide;
So may we closely walk with God,
  And feel Him ever nigh,
To keep us safe from ev'ry snare,
  To list our ev'ry cry.

And when we wrestle at the throne
  In lowly, earnest prayer,
May God us bless, and make our hearts
  To burn within us there
With holy love to Christ our Lord,
  Who taught us all to pray,
Who to the precious mercy-seat
  Is the true, living Way.

Who can describe the blessedness
  Of kneeling at the throne,
Of pouring out our souls to God
  When we are *all alone;*

'Tis sweet to hold commune with Him,
   To raise the heart in prayer
In the still, lonely midnight hour,
   When He alone is near.

And, though an answer be delayed,
   Oh! let us never faint,
But persevere, and in God's time
   An answer will be sent;
For He doth love our faith to try,
   To have us alway pray,
To wait on Him unceasingly,
   That in Him trust we may.

Let us draw very near to God,
   And He'll to us draw nigh,
He will us comfort and sustain,
   Our ev'ry want supply;
Then let us near to Jesus live,
   And through Him near the throne,
In constant converse with our God,
   We ne'er can feel alone.

June 23, 1861.

A RAINY DAY.

 RAINY day is dark and dreary,
Making lone hearts sad and weary ;
Beclouded is the azure sky,
Nought, nought but gloom can we descry.

How cheerless is a rainy day,
The sun puts forth no gladd'ning ray,
All Nature wears a darksome shroud,
While torrents pour from ev'ry cloud.

Thus oft the dark clouds veil our sky,
Of stern and chill adversity,
Investing all around with gloom,
Like that which shrouds the lonesome tomb.

Then sad and heavy is our heart,
No light can e'en a friend impart,
We must aye look beyond the cloud,
Where shines that Sun which knows no shroud !

July 14, 1861.

STANZA.

F youthful *Spring* no blossoms bring,
 Bright, *Summer* ne'er can be,
Nor *Autumn* blest, nor peace nor rest
 Shall e'er our *Winter* see.

But if youth's *Spring* fair blossoms bring,
 Its *Summer* will be gay,
Its *Autumn* bright, no darksome night
 Shall gloom its *Winter* day.

August 5, 1861.

"FEAR NOT."

DOST thou see yon little bark
Tossing 'mid the billows dark ?
Shall it ever see the land ?
Can it reach the peaceful strand ?

See the waters round it rise !
See the black as midnight skies !
See the lightning's vivid flash !
Hear the thunder's awful crash !

Yet the storm it will outride,
For it hath a skilful guide,
Safe 'twill reach the port at last,
All its toils and dangers past.

Thus it is, my soul, with thee,
Struggling o'er life's stormy sea,
Waves may dash and winds may roar,
Yet thou 'lt gain the longed-for shore.

Jesus will o'er life's dark sea
Ever Pilot be to thee,
Fear not, then, the darkest hour,
Trust, *oh ! trust His* love and power.

What though billows round thee roll !
Jesus can their rage control,
He can ev'ry tempest still,
Winds and waves obey His will. '

He but whispers, "It is I,
Why so fearful ? *I* am nigh."
Then the winds and billows cease,
Then the storm is hush'd to peace.

Safe He'll bring thee to that shore
Where all's calm for evermore !
Where no tempest e'er can rise !
Where are bright and cloudless skies !

August 16, 1861.

WHAT IS LIFE?

 H ! what is life ? a scene of strife,
  A short, a passing dream,
A lightning flash, a thunder crash,
  A silent, onward stream.

A summer shower, a fading flower,
  Which passes swift away,
A sunny gleam, a golden beam,
  Which purples dawning day.

A gloomy shroud, a darksome cloud
  Which veils a sunlit day,
A vision bright, a meteor light
  Which lures but to betray.

A journey drear, a changing year,
  Whose seasons fast decay,
A dew-drop bright, a cheerless night
  Which ends in Glory's Day.

A day of grace, a short, swift race,
  Then speed on ! why delay ?
A battle brief, a vale of grief,
  With scarce one cheering ray.

Ah! such is life! but there's a *life*
Which ne'er shall know decay,
The bliss, the love of Heaven above
Can never pass away!

September 10, 1861.

HYMN FOR CHILDREN.

IFE 'S but a Year, a *changeful* Year,
  Whose seasons swift decay,
From *Spring-time* glad, to *Winter* sad,
  All, all do pass away.

But there 's a Year, a *changeless* Year,
  That ne'er shall know decay,
A *long* New Year in yonder sphere
  That ne'er shall pass away.

Spring reigneth there ! all 's bright and fair
  In yonder world of joy,
No *Autumn* sere, no *Winter* dreár
  Shall e'er its bloom destroy.

Then may our *Spring* fair blossoms bring,
  That *Summer* gáy may be,
Our *Autumn* bright, that no dark night
  Our *Winter* e'er may see.

And when at last that *Winter 's* past,
  Calm fall asleep may we,
Till endless Spring, Life, Glory bring,
  And Immortality !

September 26, 1861.

ACROSTIC.

TO A FRIEND.

OYFUL in Jesus alway be,
    O ! cling to Him, He loveth thee,
    H appy art thou, work, watch, and pray,
    'N eath His smile tread the narrow way.

R un ! rest not in thine heavenward race,
O n ! till thou rest in God's embrace,
B right thy homeward path be ever !
I f cloudlets gloom, fear, faint, ah, never !
N ought e'er from *Jesus* can thee sever !

September 30, 1861.

ACROSTIC

R, EAR ! rear the banner of the cross !
O count all things for *Jesus* loss,
B right be thy life's swift fleeting day,
E 'en though dark cloudlets gloom thy way;
R est, rest in Jesus' fond embrace,
T ill finish'd is thine upward race

N e'er daunted be, though foes assail,
I n *Jesus'* strength thou *shalt* prevail;
S till onward to thy home above,
B eneath thy Father's eye of love,
E re long thou shalt His glory see,
T hou 'lt *like Him, with Him* ever be !

October 19, 1681.

TO JEANIE.

ARK! hark! dear friend, another year
Of thy short, passing, sojourn here,
·Hath sped away on lightning wing:
Oh! may it deep reflection bring.

Fleeter and fleeter speeds each year,
Then onward haste, and banish fear;
Each year but takes thee nearer home,
That home from which thou ne'er shalt roam.

For soon this world will pass away;—
All seasons change and swift decay;
And man is but a fading flower,
The creature of a fleeting hour.

Then pause on this thy natal day,
And think how love hath sunn'd thy way;
Till now, dear friend, thy God hath been
Thy Refuge in each wintry scene.

His gentle hand, from day to day,
Hath led thee on in life's rough way;
Then, for the future, trust His love,
E'en till thou rest in Heaven above.

May not much sorrow, care, nor strife,
Be mingled in thy cup of life ;
Yet clouds *will* gather, storms arise,
And darkness shroud the brightest skies.

But, 'mid the gloom, thou mayst descry,
With faith's all-piercing eagle eye,
Thy Better Sun still shining bright—
This changes darkness into light.

Like as a calm and placid lake
Is rippled, if a stone you take
And cast it on its sleeping breast—
Now there is unrest where was rest.

'Tis but the *surface* that is so,
All's calm down in the depths below ;
With thee, dear friend, thus may it be,
May no small cross e'er ruffle thee.

Like to a river, resting never,
Flow may thy peace, and deepen ever,
Till, lost in ocean's mighty breast,
Thy soul shall taste *eternal* rest !

November 8, 1861.

ACROSTIC.

AIL! honoured servant of the Lord,
O n! on! nor fear the foeman's sword,
R ejoice that Jesus fights with thee,
A nd in His might thou 'lt victor be :
T he crown ere long shall wreathe thy brow,
I n Heaven with Him rest, reign shalt thou ;
U p! prayer will keep thine armour bright,
S oldier of Christ! brave, fight the fight!

B lest in thy flock, they blest in thee,
O h! may ye fellow-soldiers be!
N ought e'er from *Jesus* can you sever ;
A mid all perils, fear then never!
R ally ye round His banner ever!

November 26, 1861.

THE NEW LIFE.

O live *for* Jesus ! *happy* life !
To be a wrestler in the strife,
In this the world's dark battle-field,
'Neath Him to fight, my glorious Shield :
Now militant, what need I fear ?
Triumphant day swift draweth near,
When I shall wear, beyond the tomb,
The crown of amaranthine bloom !

To live *to* Jesus ! *holy* life !
With heav'nly joy and rapture rife ;
To walk with Him in commune sweet,
To kiss the rod when He sees meet :
His grace, His wondrous love proclaim,
And spread the Rose of Sharon's fame ;
The sinner warn, the mourner cheer,
And wipe away the orphan's tear.

To live *like* Jesus ! *peaceful* life !
Calm amid the bitterest strife,
A loving friend, a generous foe,
Diffusing peace where'er I go :
Aye doing good, in prayer oft,
Averting wrath with answer soft
Frequenting oft the house of woe,
Forgiving e'en my deadliest foe.

To live *in* Jesus ! *rapturous* life !
To dwell in love, secure from strife ;
Unceasingly to feel Him near,
To enjoy His presence without fear ;
To know I 'm His, and He is mine,
In Him complete, as branch and vine ;
For were we severed, I am dead—
Strength, peace, and joy for ever fled.

To live *with* Jesus ! *blissful* life !
Beyond this scene of toil and strife ;
Day reigneth *there !* no darksome night
Shall fall on *that* land ever bright :
Loud hallelujahs I shall raise,
In songs of ceaseless, endless praise,
To Him who, on that radiant throne,
Once died to make me all His own !

December 13, 1861.

TO A FRIEND.

HILST time is thine, its hours redeem,
I mprove its moments ever !
L ife then shall be a summer's day,
L ight, love, shall sun it ever !
I f e'er a dark cloud gloom thy sky,
A h ! list the whisper, " It is I ; "
M ay dark thy path be never !

R edeem the time, it passeth swift ;
O n ! on ! it speedeth ever !
S ilent, on noiseless wing it fleets,
S till onward, slumbering never !

December 26, 1861.

THOUGHTS FOR NEW-YEAR'S DAY.

HE " Time is short ! " day after day
On lightning wing speeds fast away,
Soon will its swift career be o'er,
Its short reign ended evermore !

The " Time is short ! " haste ! sinner, haste !
Life's golden moments do not waste :
Hark ! Jesus calls—why, why delay ?
Oh ! come to Him, e'en NOW, TO-DAY !

The " Time is short ! " enter the Ark !
Lo ! tempests rage, and skies are dark ;
Oh ! enter in, while yet there's room,
In ! in ! escape the sinner's doom.

The " Time is short ! " come, trembler, come,
Make Jesus' loving breast thy home,
Life, peace, and joy He'll give to thee ;
Oh ! cling to Him, He'll faithful be.

The " Time is short ! " cheer ! mourner, cheer !
Soon dried shall be each falling tear ;
The ties that now on earth are riven
Shall reunited be in Heaven !

The " Time is short ! " on ! pilgrim, on !
Oh, linger not till life be done !
With girded loins, and staff in hand,
Press forward to Emmanuel's Land.

The " Time is short ! " speed on ! speed on !
Run, rest not till the goal be won !
Till, wreathed a victor in the strife,
Thou wear the radiant crown of life !

The " Time is short ! " work, watch, and pray,
Work now ! while it is called " to-day : "
Watch ! foes are nigh, ne'er slothful be—
Pray ! God will hear and answer thee.

The " Time is short ! " its hours redeem !
God's glory thou thy work esteem ;
His love proclaim with earnest breath,
And " be thou faithful unto death."

The " Time is short ! " oh, live to God,
Nor fear affliction's chast'ning rod,
'Tis wielded by the hand of love,
To win the heart to joys above.

The " Time is short ! " day is at hand,
Night 's known not in the " Better Land ; "
Clouds, darkness, all shall pass away
Before Heaven's bright, effulgent day !

The " Time is short ! " death 's at the door !
Up, spread thy wings ! to glory soar !
" Excelsior " thy motto be,
E'en till Heaven's pearly gates thou see.

The " Time is short ! " years roll on years,
And pass as swift as childhood's tears ;
But, ah ! with import deep they 're fraught—
The Judge of all forgets them not.

The " Time is short ! " dawn shall that day
When heavens and earth shall pass away ;
The morning breaks ! night's shadows flee !—
Time 's pass'd into Eternity !

January 1, 1862.

ODE TO THE PAST YEAR.

NOTHER year hath swiftly sped,
Numbering many with the dead !
The rich, the poor, the young, the old,
Are sleeping in death's embrace cold.
Ah ! whither has the Old Year gone
Now that its short swift race is run ?
Fled upwards to God's holy throne,
A faithful record to make known
Of time mis-spent, of thoughts unclean,
Of words and actions stained with sin.
Oh ! guilty man ! where would'st thou be,
Did not thy Saviour plead for thee ?
Oh ! may He cleanse thee from thy sins,
As now a glad New Year begins.
The past Year's dead—a New Year's born,
May Peace and Love its days adorn,
Spent in God's fear, 'twill happy be,
Each day shall glide on tranquilly.

January 5, 1862.

TO LIZZIE.

 *SPRING* has come and gone, Lizzie !
   Since thy last natal day ;
Its blossoms fair, its balmy air,
   Have passèd all away.

A *Summer's* come and gone, Lizzie !
   With all its flow'rets gay,
When Nature wears her brightest smile,
   That, too, hath pass'd away.

An *Autumn's* come and gone, Lizzie !
   When flow'rets swift decay,
When waving fields rich harvests yield,
   That, too, hath pass'd away.

A *Winter's* come and going, Lizzie !
   Whose short'ning, cheerless day
Doth make the lone heart feel so sad,
   That, too, shall pass away.

What season now is thine, Lizzie ?
   Spring ! hopeful, joyous, bright—
Just blushing into Summer-time,
   In happy, calm delight.

Then let thy youthful *Spring*, Lizzie !
Put forth its blossoms gay ;
All beauteous will thy *Summer* be,
A long, bright, sunny day.

Thine *Autumn* blest shall be, Lizzie !
Its ofttimes sadd'ning days
Shall useful, peaceful glide away,
Spent to thy Saviour's praise.

And when chill *Winter* comes, Lizzie !
When silver'd is thine hair,
May sunshine aye around thee play—
A bright smile may'st thou wear.

When *Winter's* nigh a close, Lizzie !
The soul upon the wing,
May thou, like *Summer's* setting sun,
A halo round thee fling.

Thy sun will set but here, Lizzie !
To rise in glory bright,
For, ah ! it shall no more go down—
In Heaven there is no night.

Oh ! may we there all meet, Lizzie !
And Jesus' glory share,
Is, on thy gladsome natal day,
Thine own fond Mother's prayer.

January 13, 1862.

ACROSTIC.

OY in the Lord, He is thy Stay,
E ach day He'll bless thee ever!
M ay many sunny years be thine,
I   n Jesus rest thou ever!
M uch good may'st thou be spared to do,
A nd peaceful be thou ever!

C ast on the Lord thine ev'ry care,
U pon His breast lean ever!
N e'er gloomy be thy pathway home,
N or darksome be it ever!
I   n Jesus trust, He keepeth thee,
N or will He leave thee ever!
G od is thy Refuge and thy Strength,
H e'll guide, He'll keep thee ever!
A nd till thou rest in Heaven above,
M ay He thy Sun be ever!

January 24, 1862.

ACROSTIC.

ROUND thee are the arms of love,
G   od is thy Refuge ever !
N   e'er will He leave thee, He is Love,
E   'en till thou reach thy home above,
S   torms shall assail thee never !

C   ling then to Jesus, He is nigh,
U   p ! hasten homeward ever !
'N   eath His fond eye thou 'lt alway be,
N   ow linger, slumber never !
I   n storm and calm, in sun or shade,
N   ought e'er shall move thee ever !
G   od's grace sufficient is for thee,
H   e will forsake thee never !
A   ll through this dreary, darksome vale,
M   ay He bless, keep thee ever !

January 31, 1862.

LIFE.

H ! what is Life ? a *fading flower*,
Which blooms but to decay,
Let but the chill wind on it breathe,
That *flower* hath pass'd away.

Ah ! what is Life ? a *summer shower*,
Which clouds the landscape gay,
But suddenly the sun shines out,
That *shower* hath pass'd away.

Ah ! what is Life ? a *silent stream*,
Which flows swift day by day,
Till in the depth of Ocean's breast
That *stream* hath pass'd away.

Ah ! what is Life ? a *pleasing dream*,
Which leads the soul astray ;
Too late it wakes, alas ! to find
That *dream* hath pass'd away.

Ah ! what is Life ? a *sighing wind*,
Which weeps a low, sad lay ;
We list its strains, when lo ! they cease—
That *wind* hath pass'd away.

Ah ! what is Life ? a *golden beam*,
    Which purples dawning day,
Yet oft, ere noon, a cloudlet glooms,
    That *beam* hath pass'd away.

Ah ! what is Life ? a *meteor gleam*,
    Which lures but to betray,
We gaze—when suddenly, alas !
    That *gleam* hath pass'd away.

Ah ! what is Life ? a *fleeting breath*, .
    Which lasteth but a day,
It may be ere the morrow dawn
    That *breath* hath pass'd away.

Ah ! such is Life ! but there's a *Life*
    Which ne'er shall know decay ;
The Life that Jesus gives to us
    Can never pass away !

February 15, 1862.

ACROSTIC.

TO AUNTIE MARGARET.

 AY many happy years be thine,
A nd peaceful be thou ever !
R est in the Lord, He cares for thee—
G od will forsake thee never !
A round thee are the arms of love,
R ejoice, and glad be ever !
E 'en till thou reach thy home above,
T hy path be darksome never !

S mooth may the Stream of Life flow on,
A s *on* it will glide ever !
W ith silent speed it stealeth on,
E ach moment hasting ever !
R ush on it shall till Ocean's breast
S hall it embrace for ever !

February 20, 1862.

ACROSTIC.

ARTH and its joys shall pass away,
U   pward gaze thou ever !
P   ant after God and heavenly joys,
H   aste on, and linger never !
E   re long thou 'lt reach the " Better Land,"
M   ay bright thy path be ever !
I   t must be so with Jesus nigh,
A   h ! there can clouds be never !

S   till trust in Him, He is thy Friend,
A   nd will thy Rock be ever !
W   hen tempests rise, oh ! cling to Him.
E   'en now, dismayed be never !
R   epose in Jesus' deathless love,
S   o shalt thou calm be ever !

February 28, 1862.

THE CLOUD.

 EVOTED, faithful, fond, and true,
As ever youthful hearts could be ;
Herbert—brave, manly, noble, strong,
Ethel—sweet type of modesty.

Confiding in each other's love,
All peacefully their days pass'd on,
One cloud alone obscured their sky—
That cloud dispelled, they would be one.

Consent she would not to be his,
Till in their faith they could agree ;
The path of duty she preferred
To that of pleasure, as we 'll see.

They parted—to an alien shore
He hied him, seeking peace in vain ;
Amid the gay, the giddy throng,
Oft sicken did his heart with pain.

He thought of her, so gentle, good,
Making home so cheerful, happy,
Fulfilling calm life's duties there,
So lily-like in purity.

Time passèd on—yet came he not;
Ethel grew pensive, wept alone—
She of her absent one oft thought,
Wonder'd if e'er she 'd be his own.

She ne'er forgot him in her prayers ;
She drooped and faded day by day,
For " Hope deferred makes sick the heart ;"
She mourned her loved one far away.

Oh ! was he still in thraldom bound ?
Or had the Truth now made him free ?
Could she but know ! she could but trust
That soon her prayers would answered be.

Years rolled away—he sighed for home—
Back to his friends at last he came,
A changèd man ? would it were so !
But older grown, his heart the same.

They met—anxious she scann'd his face,
Her heart thrilled at his accents mild ;
Had he his galling fetters burst ?
Was Herbert now a ransomed child ?

How oft she watched him as he sat,
Enwrapt in thought, ill, ill at ease !
Could she but heal his rankling wounds,
And to his restless soul speak peace !

Jesus alone could speak that word,
Alone could that dark cloud dispel,
Then did she flee anew to *Him*
Whose changelsss love nought e'er can quell.

Her cry was heard, her faith was proved;
The answer given : how, when, and where ?
God's time had come : we now shall see
How Jesus answered Ethel's prayer.

It was the stilly midnight hour,
When all is hushed in tranquil rest,
That hour by guilty man most feared,
That hour by saintly man lov'd best.

Dark was the night, the rain fell fast,
Low moaned the wind adown the vale ;
Each with the other vied who would
Most boist'rous be—the rain, the gale.

When in a moment, lo ! both paused,
A death-like silence reigned around,
When suddenly a voice was heard,
A voice of more than mortal sound.

Ethel—awoke from sleep, did hear
A *Father's* voice in that dread crash,
She felt no fear, she did not pale,
As, calm, she saw the lightning flash.

Kept by her Father's mighty power,
Safe in the hollow of His hand,
Peaceful was she, for well she knew
The storm would cease at *His* command.

Herbert—aroused from troublèd sleep,
How did he hear that voice o'erhead ?
His very heart grew sick from fear,
He trembling lay, o'ercome with dread.

He dared not think of that great God,
Whose will the elements obey.
He knew Him not but as that Judge
At whose bar he should stand one day.

But what proclaimed that solemn voice?
"Prepare, prepare to meet thy God!
The bed of death is spread for thee—
Soon shalt thou sleep beneath the sod."

Ethel—confiding, upward glanced,
Met her loved Father's gentle eye,
On His fond bosom laid her head—
Happy to live, happy to die.

Herbert—in anguish and dismay,
First closed his eyes, then stopped his ears;
He could not list that awful voice—
It filled his guilty soul with fears.

Why was it so? 'twas that he heard
A silent monitor within—
A " still small voice," none can elude—
Revealing all his guilt and sin.

It bade him flee to Christ, the Ark,
That there from storms he'd shelter'd be;
He entered in—a pardoned one,
A child to all eternity!

Ne'ermore feared he God's solemn voice,
Ne'ermore feared he the tempest wild;
For it was now a *Father's* voice,
And He was now His loving *child*.

After that pause, the rain, the wind,
Renewed their angry, clam'rous strife,
Till morning dawned, calm, sunny, bright—
Meet emblem of the Christian Life!

Now they are one in heart and soul,
Their hopes, their aims, their prospects one!
Ethel her hand to Herbert gives,
Vows to be his till life is done.

Now hand in hand they journey on
All through this darksome vale of tears,
Right onward to their happy home,
Their love increasing with their years.

Blest in each other's holy love,
Perpetual sunshine gilds their way,
Yet ne'er will they forget that storm
Which usher'd in a radiant day.

March 8, 1862.

BIRTHDAY THOUGHTS.

 NOTHER year of sickness
Hath slowly pass'd away,
And I am spared once more to see
Another natal day.

Throughout the bygone year
Much suff'ring has been mine,
Much sorrow, sickness, and much pain,
Yet I do not repine.

My heart and soul to God
I dedicate anew,
Oh! may He give me daily strength
My journey to pursue.

He, till now hath led me,
And He will lead me still,
Should greater suff'ring be my lot,
I'll bear my Father's will.

The cup which He has given
I'll drink most cheerfully,
Yea, to the very dregs I will,
'Tis full of love for me.

M

No wrath is in that cup,
Bitter soe'er it be,
'Tis mingled by a Father's hand,
Who careth still for me.

My life from early morn
Has been a rainy day,
And will be so till shades of even
Fall on my lonesome way.

A sunbeam now and then
Doth flit across my path,
Reminding me that " God is Love,"
That darkness is not wrath.

Ah ! no, a rainy day
Doth fertilise the soil,
Doth make the seed rich produce yield,
Rewarding man for toil.

So with adversity,
It purifies the heart,
It makes the heav'nly graces grow,
And beauty doth impart.

Not so prosperity,
It too oft proves a snare
To lead the soul away from God,
I would of it beware.

Constant sunshine dazzles,
Without the rain or dew
Soon would the seed sown wither, die,
Which no Spring can renew.

My children are the tie
Which binds my soul to earth,
I pray that I may sparèd be
To hail their second birth.

How many a chink's been made
In this frail house of clay,
By sickness in the year now gone,
Soon will it fall away.

Then will the soul escape,
And joyful mount on high,
To take possession of that home
Prepared beyond the sky.

" God's House !" all there is joy,
No sickness, sorrow, care,
Can darken that bright, holy home—
All, all is sunshine there.

What matter, then, the clouds
Of this short fleeting life,
When we think on what's reserved for those
Who conquer in the strife !

I am not far from home,
It neareth day by day ;
May Jesus be my Light, my Sun,
Through all life's tearful way.

And when the battle's o'er,
I'll lay my weapons down,
For warfare, quiet rest enjoy,
And for the Cross, the Crown.

God bless me day by day,
And then I shall be blest,
God keep my soul in perfect peace,
Till I in glory rest.

March 19, 1862.

TO TOM.

NOTHER year has sped, my boy,
  For ever fled away,
And thou art spared once more to see
  Thy happy natal day.

With lively gratitude, my boy,
  Be thine heart filled alway
To God, who through the bygone years
  Hath kept thee day by day.

Oh ! give to Him thine heart, my boy,
  Love Him in life's fresh *morn*,
Then will its *noon* be all serene—
  Light shall its *night* adorn.

Remember that His eye, my boy,
  Is ever bent on thee ;
To do what's right He will thee aid,
  Then never troublèd be.

Life's duties may be hard, my boy,
  Life's trials bitter be,
Thy pathway through this changing scene
  May desert seem to thee.

But if in this thy youth, my boy,
Thou giv'st thyself to God,
Jesus, thy Better Sun, shall shine
On all thy homeward road.

Should snares beset thy path, my boy,
Temptations thee assail,
Seek strength from God in earnest prayer,
And o'er them thou 'lt prevail.

Walk humbly with thy God, my boy,
Love mercy, justly do,
Then will He aid and strengthen thee
Thy journey to pursue.

That day remembered is, my boy,
Forgot it ne'er can be,
When thou to me by God wast given,
Thy mother welcomed thee.

She gave thee then to God, my boy,
Asked Him thy Friend to be,
Thy Portion sure, that He would be
A *Father* unto thee.

Hath He not heard her prayer, my boy?
Ah ! yes, He 'll yet thee bless ;
He 'll give thee grace to trust in Him,
To grow in holiness.

Oh ! come to Jesus *now*, my boy,
He loves the youthful heart ;
Devote to Him thy life, thine all,
And peace He will impart.

Long mayest thou sparèd be, my boy,
  A useful life be thine,
Spent in God's fear, in doing good,
  His love on thee shall shine.

And when life's journey 's o'er, my boy,
  May Jesus welcome thee
To His house of many mansions,
  His glory there to see.

One anxious, fond request, my boy,
  I make to thee this day;
Me seek to meet at God's *right* hand,
  When Time hath passed away.

May we all meet in Heaven, my boy,
  Ne'er more to parted be,
To sing the rapturous, triumph song
  Through all eternity.

God bless thee *now*, mine own dear boy,
  God give thee peace for ever,
God lift on thee His gracious face,
  God keep thy soul for ever.

April 17, 1862.

PERFECT PEACE.

ROUND her couch they're watching
  With earnest, anxious eye,
In which a tear-drop trembles,
  For fear that she may die.

Hush'd is each noisome footfall,
  Suppress'd is every breath,
Exchang'd are tearful glances,
  Ah ! sure, can this be death ?

She seemeth calmly sleeping,
  That mother young and fair,
Her count'nance, oh ! how radiant,
  No trace of sorrow there.

That sleep, oh ! how deceitful !
  Death's dews are on her brow,
That sleep which knows no waking
  Is stealing o'er her now.

She's in the arms of Jesus,
  Her pillow is His breast,
As babe on mother's bosom,
  So tranquil is her rest.

He 's come to take this Lily,
   In Eden bowers to bloom,
By His fond hand transplanted
   From this dark valley-gloom.

He, with love ineffable,
   Has come to take her home,
She hears the angel's welcome,
   " Come ! sister spirit, come !"

E'en now she hears the music
   Of that seraphic band,
E'en now she sees the beauty
   Of that bright, happy land.

But ere earth's ties are riven,
   Ere yet she falls asleep,
Here meek eyes once more open,
   As if to say, " Why weep ?"

Her little ones are kneeling,
   They heave a heavy sigh,
They gaze on that fond mother,
   They meet her gentle eye.

A fond farewell it smileth,
   So tender and so sweet ;
Ah ! sure that beauteous flow'ret
   Is for God's garden meet.

To each lov'd one it seemeth,
   As if some angel-band
Was calling that sweet mother
   Up to the spirit-land.

She closed her eyes so gently,
　So calmly fell asleep,
That oh! it were but sinful
　To murmur or to weep.

Home she has gone with Jesus,
　Her sufferings now are o'er;
With Him she is rejoicing,
　To weep, ah, never more!

Then, lov'd ones, stay your weeping,
　Your loss is but her gain;
If ye are one in Jesus,
　Soon shall ye meet again.

She waits—that Angel-Mother,
　In bliss before the throne,
To welcome you to glory,
　Whene'er your work is done.

Think of that joyous meeting,
　Think desert trials o'er,
Think of that happy greeting,
　Think of the "Evermore."

That blissful time is nearing,
　'Tis on the wing alway;
Night's shades are surely falling—
　Soon break will Glory's Day.

That Day which knows no ending,
　That Day of perfect light,
That Day all days transcending,
　That Day which knows no night!

April 26, 1862.

ALICE.

HE rose may bloom upon the cheek, whilst
    death is at the core ;
The smile may play around the lips, whilst
    yet the heart is sore.

And so it is—that loved one droops, the rose pales on
    her cheek ;
Hers is a grief, a ceaseless grief, she not a tear can
    weep.

Her sorrow is too deep for tears, her sad and sparkless
    eye
Bespeaks the anguish of her heart, the fount of tears is
    dry.

Ah ! yes ; deep is the bitter grief that weighs upon her
    heart,
But yet her look of calm plain shows she feels
    affliction's smart.

Not only feels, but owns it too ; she knows it is her
    God,
Who doeth all things wisely, well, who holds the
    chast'ning rod.

She kisses it—it is stretchèd forth by her kind Father's
hand,
She meekly bends beneath its weight, it is at *His*
command.

She murmurs not, ah! no; she joys to tread in Jesus'
path,
To drink of the cup whereof He drank, for there's in
hers no wrath.

Ah! no; 'twas love that mingled it, bitter soe'er it be,
Then to the dregs she will it drink, patient, aye
cheerfully.

For why? her loving Saviour is her Husband, Portion,
Friend,
What wonder, then, she peaceful is—her griefs with life
will end.

She knows that in a happier land, all desert trials o'er,
She'll meet again the loved, not lost—not lost, *but* gone
before.

For loving ones enslaved in sin, still doth she hope and
pray,
That God would lead them to the fold, from which
they're far away.

This hope sustains her bleeding heart, she knows to
whom she prays;
Her Saviour is her All in All, her hopes on Him she
stays.

She sits, like Mary, at His feet—like John, leans on His
  breast,
Thus calm she treads life's rugged path, for *He* has
  given her rest.

Life's daily duties she performs, as 'neath her Father's
  eye,
She walks with Him in lowliness, her thoughts are
  fix'd on high.

She knows that when her hour is come, she'll pass
  from earth away,
That when for glory she is meet, she'll soar to endless
  day.

To be for ever with the Lord, to see Him face to face,
To bask beneath His eye of love, to rest in His
  embrace.

One hour of such ecstatic bliss, all griefs will be forgot,
Or be but dim rememberings, not worth a passing
  thought.

Not once are they to be compared with the deep joy of
  Heaven,
" With the exceeding weight of glory," to God's own
  children given.

Such bright hopes cheer her anguished heart, impart a
  healing balm,
No wonder then she peaceful is, so gentle, cheerful,
  calm.

Each step she takes she neareth home, her heart is there
e'en now ;
She breathes the very air of Heaven, its peace is on her
brow.

She waiteth at its portals bright, she feels they 'll soon
unclose,
And give her evermore to taste its deep, its full repose.

Well may she wait, fulness of joy shall soon be hers for
ever ;
Her present griefs will but enhance her bliss, which end
shall never !

ARRAN, *May* 24, 1862.

TO MARY.

NOTHER year has circled round,
  Time fleeteth fast away ;
The first of June has dawned again,
  Thy gladsome natal day.

And with it many loving friends
  Good wishes wish for thee ;
But than thy mother, Mary dear,
  None can so heartily.

Though bitter oft's the cup of life,
  With sweets may thine be filled ;
May no deep grief e'er wound thine heart,
  If so thy God hath willed.

It may be that a bitter draught
  Be needed discipline ;
If so, oh drink it patiently,
  Ne'er murmur nor repine.

Thou art of age this festal morn,
  Thy steps may wisdom guide,
That bright may be thy day of life,
  And calm thine eventide.

Like to a dark receding wall, •
  The future is to thee;
But fear it not, in Jesus trust,
  He will thy Guardian be.

Thou hast a loving daughter been,
  Most dutiful to me;
Hast cheered mine heart in many an hour
  Of drear adversity.

Thou rainbowed hast each darkling cloud,
  With thy fond, loving smile;
Then be to me a sunbeam still,
  Through all my little while.

Thine be a happy prosp'rous lot,
  A long, bright summer's day,
And when shall fall the shades of eve,
  Calm mayst thou pass away!

To bloom in amaranthine bowers,
  With loved ones gone before,
And by the Tree of Life to rest,
  And joy for evermore!

There may we meet, my Mary dear,
  Ne'ermore to part for ever!
For oh! it were sad, sad indeed,
  Did death life's friendships sever!

Thy mother's blessing's thine this day,
  God's blessing thine be ever!
May sunshine gild thine earthly path,
  Dark shadows gloom it never!

June 1, 1862.

ACROSTIC.

TO A FRIEND.

MID the changeful scenes of life,
N ought e'er can move the ever !
N or sun, nor shade can ruffle thee,
E ach day thou 'rt peaceful ever !

B ecause in Jesus thou art safe,
E 'en storms can harm thee never !
V ictor, through Him, o'er ev'ry foe,
E re long thou 'lt reign for ever !
R adiant shall be thy crown of life,
I n Heaven thou 'lt sorrow never !
D arkness and clouds are known not there,
G od is its Sun, all 's bright and fair,
E nduring, changeless, ever !

June 18, 1862.

YONDER.

IST to the Sabbath-bells of Heaven
　　Stealing softly on the ear,
　　Pealing from the heights of glory,
　　Cheering weary pilgrims here.

Those sweet bells are ever ringing,
　　List their soft angelic strain,
" Blessing, honour, power, and glory,
　　To the Lamb that once was slain."

Earth ! echo back this song of glory,
　　Let thy Sabbath-bells resound,
Till, in all nations under Heaven
　　Shall be heard their gladd'ning sound.

Sufferer ! on that bed of anguish,
　　Tossing day and night from pain,
Hark ! the heav'nly bells are sounding,
　　" Here thou 'lt ne'er be sick again."

Mourner ! o'er thy rosebuds weeping,
　　Sweet to thee their soothing strain,
" Here thou 'lt find thy cherish'd treasures,
　　Here thou 'lt never weep again."

Pilgrim ! weary, by sin burdened,
  Soiled thy robe with many a stain,
Sweet to hear that heav'nly music,
  " Here thou 'lt never sin again."

Ceaseless are those chimes of glory,
  Sounding forth Jehovah's praise,
And from golden harps the sainted
  Sweetest strains to Jesus raise.

May we, Sabbath-bells of glory,
  Ever hear your joyous strain,
In triumphant tones proclaiming,
  " Here doth Jesus ever reign."

July 13, 1862.

ACROSTIC.

FOR BAZAAR.

ESTOW your kindly aid on me,
U p! friends, and help me cheerfully,
R eseat me, lend a helping hand,
N or let me thus neglected stand,
T ime, with his touch, has told on me
I ndelibly, as you may see;
S o pity me, and give your aid,
L et all within me new be made,
A nd deeply grateful I shall be,
N or ever doubt my constancy;
D ismiss not, then, my humble plea.

C ome! enter in, welcome are all,
H ere is the good seed sown;
U nto all who obey my call,
R edemption is made known;
C ome! freed awhile from toil and strife,
H ear of " The Way, the Truth, the Life."

BURNTISLAND, *August* 22, 1862.

THE STORM-VOICE.

HEREFORE should the Christian
tremble
When he sees the lightning-flash ?
Wherefore should he fear and quake
When he lists the thunder-crash ?

'Tis but his *Father's* voice he hears,
Speaking to his awe-struck soul,
A God of might but yet of love,
Who'll the tempest's rage control.

His *Father's* voice ! then why afraid,
When he knows that Father's near ?
O'ershadowed by His wings of love,
Can he feel a shade of fear ?

No ; calm he lists the angry storm,
Which is 'neath his God's control,
He has a sure, a safe retreat,
Fear, then, cannot move his soul.

And whither does the Christian flee
In that darksome, solemn hour ?
To the fond bosom of his God,
There to own His mighty power.

Calm pillow'd on that gentle breast,
    Danger ne'er can him betide,
Close folded in those tender arms,
    He in safety doth abide.

The tempest-cloud may gloom o'erhead,
    Lightnings flash and thunders roar,
A pall of silence, deadly still,
    May be spread the landscape o'er.

He heeds it not, too happy he,
    Lost in God through commune sweet,
Adoring rapture thrills his soul,
    Prostrate at the Mercy-seat.

There, in *silent* adoration,
    Near, yea, very near the throne,
He seems as if away from earth,
    And with Jesus all alone.

This is, methinks, the nearest Heaven
    He can on this earth enjoy,
Calm resting on his Father's breast,
    Nought can e'er his peace destroy.

But now the storm has spent its rage,
    Tears are sunny smiles again,
The roaring wind is lulled to rest,
    Peaceful is the billowy main.

The sun breaks forth in splendour bright,
    Brighter from the gloom before,
The landscape smiles beneath his beams—
    All is lovely, gay, once more.

And such is life! now storm, now calm,
  Meets the Christian in his path;
Now sunshine gilds each beauteous scene,
  Now the storm descends in wrath.

Steadfast is he; walking with God,
  Him nor sun nor shade can move,
In *Jesus* hid, the Rock of Ages,
  He his Joy will ever prove.

He walks by faith with Jesus now,
  Sweeter far to walk by sight
Among the verdant meads of Heaven,
  In that Home of glory bright.

There can be heard no tempest-voice,
  There the storm-cloud gloometh never!
There is a Sun that never sets,
  There beauty vernal bloometh ever!

BURNTISLAND, *Sept.* 4, 1862.

ACROSTIC.

TO A FRIEND.

J OY in the Lord, He'll be thy Friend,
    O n Him repose till life shall end,
    H is hand shall lead thee day by day,
    N e'er shalt thou stray from Wisdom's
        way.

    R un, rest not in the heav'nly race,
    A ye onward to the resting-place,
    E 'en till thou see God face to face.

October 20, 1862.

ACROSTIC.

A VOICE FROM GLORY.

HY lov'd one lives in glory, faith now is
chang'd to sight;
H ope, now, is full fruition in this bright
land of light;
O n Jesus' bosom resting, before the throne above,
'M id angels and the sainted I 'm hymning Jesus' love,
A nd, in His presence basking, I wait to welcome thee,
S oon as thy journey 's ended we 'll re-united be.

O h, then, be up and doing! Time fleeteth fast away;
L et thoughts of coming glory soothe, cheer thee on
thy way.
I taste a bliss unending, I am what thou shalt be;
V ictor o'er sin and sorrow, I Jesus' glory see.
E 'en now, by faith, behold me with golden harp in
hand,
R edeeming love I 'm chanting n this fair, happy land.

October 31, 1862.

TO JEANIE.

NOTHER fleeting year, Jeanie!
  Again has fled away,
And I am spared once more to hail
  Thy happy natal day.

How good thy God hath been, Jeanie!
  Throughout the bygone year;
A hiding-place He's been to thee,
  When storms were loud and near.

Deep gratitude be thine, Jeanie!
  For all His mercies past,
And for the future trust His love—
  Thy cares on Him all cast.

Oh! lean upon His arm, Jeanie!
  When weary and opprest,
Upon His loving breast repose,
  For He will give thee rest.

Into His gracious ear, Jeanie!
  Breathe out thine ev'ry sigh,
And with His arm encircling thee,
  No danger can come nigh.

On that fond loving breast, Jeanie!
 Weep out thine ev'ry tear,
And He, with love ineffable,
 Thy lowly plaint will hear.

Live very near the throne, Jeanie!
 No resting-place so sweet,
For there the weary laden soul
 Doth with its Saviour meet.

And there, as friend with friend, Jeanie!
 With Jesus thou mayst be ;
Alone with Him, in converse close,
 He will draw near to thee.

When thy life's day is bright, Jeanie!
 Calm, lowly shalt thou be,
For, walking humbly with thy God,
 No sun shall dazzle thee.

But should a darksome cloud, Jeanie!
 E'er gloom thy sunny sky,
To thee it will be light as day,
 Thy Better Sun is nigh,

To cheer thy drooping heart, Jeanie!
 To dry thy glistening eye,
To point thee to thy happy home,
 Prepared beyond the sky.

For there are loved ones there, Jeanie!
 Dear, dear to thee and me,
Who now have joined that ransomed throng,
 And Jesus' glory see.

And when life's day is done, Jeanie!
Thine ev'ry conflict o'er,
In Jesus' arms thou 'lt fall asleep,
To be blest evermore.

Thou art my cherish'd friend, Jeanie!
Hast been from childhood's day,
A Winter friend, faithful and true,
Thou 'st been to me alway.

And may we meet in Heaven, Jeanie!
To part and sorrow never!
But with our loved ones gone before,
To rest in Jesus ever!

November 8, 1862.

ACROSTIC.

A VOICE FROM HEAVEN.

ROUND the throne of glory, thy loved
one's basking now,
N or sin nor sorrow grieves me, Heaven's
peace is on my brow,
N e'ermore do cares annoy me, then
why so sad art thou ?

S oon as life's day is ended, we'll meet to part no more,
A nd with the holy angels, we'll Jesus' love adore,
W here'er the Lamb shall lead us, we'll follow with
delight,
E 'en now I sing His praises in this fair land of light ;
R ejoicing in His presence, I wait to welcome thee,
S till onward then to glory, soon we'll together be.

R est aye on Jesus' bosom, He'll cheer and strengthen
thee ;
U pon His arm still leaning, thou ne'er canst lonely be ;
L ist to His gentle whisper, "Thy tears I'll wipe
away,
E re long with Me in glory thou'lt rest and reign for
aye."

November 16, 1862.

FAITH.

OST thou see that rose-tree bending,
'Neath Winter's chilly blast?
She cannot raise her tiny head,
Death's pallor's o'er her cast.

Silent she weeps, her children fair,
Are fading one by one,
She, too, will droop, but not until
Her little ones are gone.

She sees them drooping hour by hour,
With watchful, mournful care,
Yet murmurs not, they will but sleep,
The germ of life's still there.

And when her last frail one is gone,
She, too, will fall asleep,
No sigh will 'scape her loving heart,
No teardrop will she weep.

She knows that when the Winter's o'er,
With beauty on her wing,
To rouse all Nature into life,
Will haste the balmy Spring.

She knows that with her little ones,
  She'll hear that joyous voice,
Inviting her to wake again,
  And with her to rejoice.

Thus hopeful, calm, she falls asleep,
  Nor fears the chilly storm;
The snow-wreath will but guard the germ—
  Protect her fragile form.

Until the breath of Spring once more
  Decks her in vernal sheen,
And Summer sees her lovelier far,
  Adorning each fair scene.

Then, Christian mother, comfort take,
  Thy rose-buds from thee riven
Shall only sleep, with thee to wake,
  And bloom more bright in Heaven!

December 14, 1862.

NEW YEAR'S HYMN.

"Yet a little while."

REJOICE! my fellow-pilgrim, pause on this festal day,
Review God's dealings with thee, ere thou resume thy way,
Think o'er thy many mercies, for good thy God hath been,
His hand till now hath led thee through ev'ry chequer'd scene.

Now sunshine and now shadow, now sickness and now health,
Now tempest and now stillness, now poverty, now wealth,
Must gild or gloom this valley, as thou dost march along,
But it can ne'er be lonely, if *Jesus* be thy song.

'Tis ofttimes toilsome, dreary, thine heart might well-nigh fail,
But for the cheering vista beyond this darksome vale.
With aching limbs and weary, still onward! ne'er delay,
The "Better Land" is nearing, where there is rest for aye.

A few more tottering footsteps, the desert will be past !
A few more weary stages, and then will come the last !
A few more burning tear-drops, then wiped shall be
thine eyes !
A few more fears and doubtings, then bright, unclouded
skies !

Rejoice ! my fellow-mariner, o'er life's unquiet sea,
Thy little bark, though fragile, can never shipwreck'd be.
By love its helm is guided, then safe 'twill reach the
shore,
Where moor'd 'twill be for ever, its weary tossings o'er.

When winds and waves are raging, when midnight is
the sky,
Soft falls the gentle whisper, " Oh ! fear not, it is I,
Thy skilful, faithful Pilot, trust Me, whate'er betide,
Thy bark, though frail and shatter'd, I'll guide to
yonder side."

Life's but a sea of troubles, swift wave succeedeth wave,
But from all rocks and quicksands thy bark will *Jesus*
save,
Then steer on ! Christian mariner, nor dread the
tempest's rage,
See yonder bow of mercy ! God will the storm assuage.

Another port is touch'd at, on this, a New Year's Day,
And reach'd may be the haven, ere this year pass away,
But if so, 'twill be joyous, all stormy tempests o'er,
Thy bark shall be at anchor on Heaven's peaceful
shore !

Rejoice! my fellow-courser, thy race is nearer run,
The goal is ever nearing, soon will the prize be won;
Though ofttimes faint and flagging, ne'er loiter in the race,
Oh! look thou unto *Jesus*, sufficient is *His* grace.

Thy path by thorns is hedgèd, to keep thee in the way,
For were it open, flowery, thou mightest go astray,
Then wing thy speed right onward, thine eye fix'd on
the prize
Awarded to each victor—a mansion in the skies!

Foes many thee encompass to lull thy soul to sleep,
And if they're not resisted, *too* late thou 'lt wake, to
weep;
Then list not their enchantments, which are a vain
dream all,
But to the bourne press forward, lest darkness o'er
thee pall.

Oh! keep thine eye on Jesus, till at the goal thou stand,
Go! win the wreath unfading from His own gracious
hand,
Then shall the welcome greet thee, "Victor o'er sin,
well done!
Rest now from all life's labours, thy crown is nobly
won!"

Rejoice, my fellow-warrior, on this world's battle-field,
Oh! fight the good fight boldly, for *Jesus* is thy shield
When foes press thick around thee, brave, fearless
ever be,
Clad in the Christian's armour, no weapons pierce can
thee.

What keepeth bright that armour? unceasing fervent
    prayer;
What nerveth thee for conflict? trust in thy Father's
    care;
Then face the fiercest battle with calm and dauntless
    brow,
And when the fight is hottest, with valour girt be thou.

What banner art thou rearing? the banner of the Cross,
For which the Christian warrior counts all things else
    but loss;
Unfurl it, wave it boldly, Love's pennon floats o'er thee,
Thy Captain fighting with thee, through *Him* thou'lt
    victor be.

And when life's battle's ended, when laid thy weapons
    down,
The Cross shall be exchangèd for the amaranthine
    Crown,
And for the sword, the palm-branch, for warfare,
    endless rest,
And for the trumpet's war-shout, the harpings of the
    Blest!

January 1, 1863.

NEW YEAR'S HYMN FOR CHILDREN

JESUS! guide a warrior band
Marching through a desert land,
Home is daily drawing near,
Past is now another year.

Jesus! be our Strength and Shield,
Guard us on the battle-field,
May Love's banner o'er us wave—
It from danger will us save.

Jesus! foes around us press
In this dreary wilderness,
But they shall before us flee,
If we put our trust in Thee.

Jesus! with Thee at our side,
Danger ne'er can us betide,
Brave and fearless we shall be,
Thou hast conquer'd, so shall *we*.

Jesus! we shall boldly fight
With our Leader full in sight,
Arm'd by prayer and nerv'd by grace,
We may fiercest battles face.

Jesus ! when our warfare's done,
Fought the fight, and glory won,
Wreathe us, victors in the strife,
With the radiant crown of life.

January 1, 1863.

TO LIZZIE.

HAT shall I say, dear Lizzie,
   On this thy natal day,
For were I now to lecture thee,
   Methinks I hear thee say—

" Mama is alway writing thus,
   And it is such a bore,"
So I shall profit by the hint,
   And do so now no more.

Thy natal day I 'll ne'er forget,
   Sad was thy Mother's heart,
But thou wert given, a sunbeam bright,
   To soothe affliction's smart.

So joyous, loving, fond art thou,
   Aye 'dutiful to me,
Dark, dreary days have brightened been,
   And still shall be by thee.

Thy lightsome footfall on the stair
   Oft makes my heart right glad,
Thy sunny smile, thy merry laugh,
   Oft cheers me when I 'm sad.

Thy loving kiss so fondly given
　　Oft soothes mine aching heart,
For thou must alway have the last
　　Whene'er we meet or part.

Mine own Benoni ever be,
　　Thy mother's darling treasure,
Thy sister and thy brother's pet,
　　Diffusing joy and pleasure.

Like the sweet lily of the vale
　　That blooms in shade unseen,
Or lowly, modest violet,
　　Beneath its refuge green.

But for the fragrance sweet diffus'd
　　Their presence is not known,
So may thy virtues, dearest one,
　　In loving deeds be shown.

That thou a halo bright may fling
　　Around thy path through life,
Which, though oft dark, still may it be
　　With many oases rife.

This ne'er-to-be-forgotten day
　　Is fraught with grief to me,
Links sever'd were which here below
　　Can ne'er united be.

And as I locked thee in mine arms
　　In solemn midnight hour,
I asked of God to make thee His,
　　Blessings on theé to shower.

And has He not my prayer heard ?
　Has He not watched o'er thee ?
Has Jesus not thy Shepherd been
　From helpless infancy ?

Ah, yes ! sweet one, the fatherless
　Do share His deepest love ;
Then trust Him, love Him more and more,
　E'en till thou rest above.

Now, dearest pet, thou wilt not say
　That I have lectured thee,
I only wish that all through life
　Thou mayest happy be.

If thou hast given thy heart to God,
　Him chosen as thy Guide,
Sunlit shall be thine homeward path,
　No ill shall thee betide.

And in the Christian's home of joy,
　When earthly days are o'er,
May we, a family of love,
　Repose for evermore.

And now adieu, mine own loved one,
　God keep thee day by day,
Beneath His shade mayest thou abide,
　Now, henceforth, and for aye !

January 13, 1863.

ACROSTIC.

TO A FRIEND.

OY in the Lord, He cares for thee,
A nd in Him calm trust ever,
M ay sunshine gild thy pathway here,
E 'en till thou reach yon happy sphere,
S ad be thine heart, ah ! never !

G ive thou to God thy Summer's prime,
O h ! love and serve Him ever !
R edeem the Time, it fleeteth fast,
D ay follows day, swift ever !
O n then, ne'er linger by the way,
'N eath Jesus' eye rest ever !

February 22, 1863.

ACROSTIC.

TO ANOTHER FRIEND.

HOW swift the stream of Time flows on !
E 'en now 'tis gliding ever!
N ought e'er can stay its silent speed,
R ush on it will, oh ! then take heed,
Y outh will not last for ever !

G od will thee bless, if thou Him serve,
O 'er thee He watcheth ever !
R est in His love, He's alway nigh,
D ark be thy sky,—ah, never !
O h ! may it aye be sunny, bright,
N e'er gloomed by cloudlets ever !

March 1, 1863.

EARTH'S CHANGES.

ETHINKS I hear a footfall
Nearing, sure but slow,
O'er hill and valley stealing,
Causing hearts to glow.

'Tis of a gentle maiden,
Lovely is her mien;
She cometh! oh, how welcome!
Deck'd in vernal green.

New life again imparting
To the sleeping earth,
Dispelling gloom and sadness,
Shedding joy and mirth.

All Nature at her summons
Wakes again to bloom,
And joyfully upspringeth
From her wintry tomb.

The husbandman, now hopeful,
Sows the precious seed;
With flow'rets gay enamell'd
Is each verdant mead.

With buds the trees are laden,
　Verdure gems the plain,
Sweet choristers re-echo
　Nature's cheerful strain.

The youthful earth rejoiceth,
　All 's with beauty rife ;
The air is balmy, healthful—
　All is joy and life.

E'en man her coming haileth,
　Health is on her wing ;
Back to the cheek so pallid
　Roses she will bring.

The little pensive snowdrop,
　Which with joy we greet,
Heralds the approaching
　Of that maiden sweet.

Then comes the modest primrose,
　With its sister-band,
Diffusing beauty, gladness—
　Bright'ning all the land.

For at her breath the streamlet
　Leaves its icy bed,
Through the vale meand'ring,
　Wakes as from the dead.

The mourner's tear she stayeth,
　Cheereth broken hearts,
And to the lonely reft one
　Solace she imparts.

To that bright world she pointeth,
   Where she ever reigns,
Where verdure never fading
   Mantles all its plains.

Then welcome, lovely maiden,
   To this land of ours,
With thy soft, healthful breezes,
   And thy fragrant flowers !

March 10, 1863.

ANTICIPATION.

LIFE'S but a Year, a *changeful* Year,
    Whose seasons fade swift ever!
A *toilsome* Year, a *fleeting* Year,
    For Time doth slumber never!

But there's a Year, a *changeless* Year,
    Whose spring-time fadeth never!
A *long New* Year, in yon bright sphere,
    Where beauty bloometh ever!

Earth's short, swift Year, oft dark and drear,
    Is speeding onward ever!
And *Heaven's New* Year is drawing near,
    That pass away shall never!

A *deathless* Year, is that *New* Year,
    For sin is known there never!
A *blissful* Year, whose bright career
    Shall circle on for ever!

A *joyful* Year, for *there* no tear
    Can dim the calm eye ever!
A *cloudless* Year, for doubt and fear
    Shall gloom its bright sky never!

A *radiant* Year is *Heaven's New* Year,
Its bright sun setteth never !
A *happy* Year is *Glory's* Year,
Its pleasures last for ever !

March 19, 1863.

TO TOM.

NOTHER year has fleeted by,
How swift the seasons pass,
Reminding us, mine own dear boy,
That we are but as grass.

But you and I have sparèd been
To see again this day,
A happy useful life be thine—
God be thy Guide alway.

With each new dawning year, my boy,
Mayst thou in wisdom grow,
A comfort be to all thy friends—
A blessing here below.

Thy God hath kept thee hitherto,
And He will keep thee still,
Give then thy youthful heart to Him,
Obey His holy will.

Think of the mercies manifold
With which He loadeth thee ,
He makes thy cup to overflow,
Then ever grateful be.

Ne'er, ne'er shall I forget that day
When thou to me wert given,
A young immortal to be reared
For happiness and Heaven.

Then may it be thine heart's desire
To be a child of God,
To tread the narrow path of life,
The path that Jesus trod.

Ah! sure thou wilt be happy, blest,
If Jesus sun thy way,
No clouds can gloom thine azure sky,
All will be one bright day.

May no harsh words escape thy lips,
No cross e'er ruffle thee,
Fear to offend in word and deed,
Aye peaceful, gentle be.

Let not the thorns and briars, my boy,
Of this dark wilderness,
Thee hinder in thy heavenward path,
But onward ever press.

This world's temptations all resist,
For it hath many a snare
To lead the young away from God,
Then, O my boy, beware!

To Jesus look in tempted hour,
He's alway at thy side,
And to withstand the wicked's wiles,
Strength needed He'll provide.

Be diligent in business still,
  As thou hast been till now,
In spirit fervent, serve the Lord,
  And peaceful be shalt thou.

Life's duties may be arduous oft,
  But Jesus will thee bless,
Will thee uphold in all thy ways,
  Will be thy Righteousness.

Still ever be, mine own lov'd boy,
  As thou hast ever been,
A loving son, a brother kind,
  Through all life's chequer'd scene.

And when shall end life's little day,
  Calm be its evening light,
In radiance may thy sun go down,
  To rise in glory bright.

To rise in yonder world of joy,
  Where all is blissful ever !
Where suns shall pale, where moons shall wane,
  Where stars shall dimm'd be never !

April 17, 1863.

ACROSTIC.

TO A FRIEND.

 OW swift the stream of time flows on !
E 'en now 'tis fleeting fast,
L ive then to God, 'and slumber never !
E ach day may be thy last,
N 'er linger then, but onward ever.

" C hanging " is stamped on all below,
R epose is known not ever !
I n Jesus only there is rest,
C an ought thee from Him sever ?
H ath He not said, " O ! cling to Me
T ill life is o'er, distrust Me never !
O n My fond bosom alway lean,
Near to My heart I 'll keep thee ever ! "

H ope then in Him, He 'll ne'er thee leave,
A nd bright be life's path ever !
I f cloudlets gloom, thy Sun descry,
N e'er fâint—dismayed be never !
E ach day but takes thee nearer home,
S erene be, happy ever !

May 16, 1863.

TO MARY.

Y Mary dear,
    Another year
On swift, still wing has sped ;
    'Tis past and gone,
    For ever flown,
How noiseless was its tread !

    Be happy, gay,
    On this bright day,
The gladsome first of June ;
    God has been good,
    May gratitude
Thy heart to praise attune.

    Should e'er a cloud
    Thy calm sky shroud,
To Jesus ever flee,
    He 's alway near
    The sad to cheer,
He will thy solace be.

    On His fond breast
    Oh ! may'st thou rest,
He loves the youthful heart,
    If thou Him seek,
    He will thee keep,
His grace to thee impart.

This vale of tears
Too oft appears
To youth a scene of joy,
But oh ! beware,
Full many a snare
May oft thy peace destroy.

But there's a life,
All free from strife,
Where nought shall e'er decay—
The life of love,
In Heaven above,
Shall never fade away.

Year rolls on year,
Tear flows on tear,
Throughout this darkling scene,
Yet in this night
Oft gleams of light
Athwart the sky are seen.

In storm and calm,
A healing balm,
May Jesus be to thee.
He'll be thy Friend
Till Time shall end,
Then thy Reward He'll be.

With all thine heart,
The Better Part,
Choose thou in youthful day,
Then will thy life
With joy be rife,
That joy which lasts for aye.

And as a rose
In beauty glows
In this sweet month of June,
So mayest thou,
With radiant brow,
In health and gladness bloom.

Sowing gladness,
Quelling sadness,
In this thy Summer-tide,
Then 'neath God's smile,
Life's little while
Away shall gently glide.

Thy future life
Be free from strife,
May no cares thee annoy,
Nor anxious fears,
Nor bitter tears—
Thine be a life of joy.

The Lord thee bless,
Give thee His peace,
My Mary dear, this day,
His blessing best
On thy head rest,
God keep thee now, alway!

June 1, 1863.

ENDURING.

E still, my soul! 'tis Jesus speaks,
It is thy growth in grace He seeks,
As now He lays thee in the dust,
'Tis that thou mayest more Him trust.

Be still, my soul! thine anxious cares,
Thine ev'ry fear thy Saviour shares,
His tears He mingles with thine own,
He lists thy sighs when all alone.

Be still, my soul! O trust His love,
He'd have thee rise and soar above,
To view with Faith's keen eagle eye
Thy happy home beyond the sky.

Be still, my soul! and kiss the rod,
'Tis wielded by the hand of God—
A Saviour-God, whose name is Love—
Who thus His children's faith doth prove.

Be still, my soul! the furnace-fire
Is not to thee a proof of ire,
'Tis but a proof of love divine,
To make thee in His likeness shine.

Be still, my soul! dost thou not know
There's nought but sorrow here below;
Joy is reserved for Heaven alone,
For there the tear-drop is unknown.

Be still, my soul! should e'er a cloud
From thy Belovèd thee enshroud,
Still trust Him, though thou canst not see,
To prove thy faith He thus tries thee.

Be still, my soul! though dark the cloud
That wraps thee be as midnight shroud,
Still doth thy Saviour smile on thee.
Then trust, O trust, ne'er faithless be.

Be still, my soul! why mournful thou?
The wherefore of God's dealings now
Thou soon shalt see; before the throne
All hidden things shall be made known.

Be still, my soul! a little while;
And thou shalt bask 'neath Jesus' smile,
Night's on the wane, soon gleams of day
Shall usher in the Far-away!

June 23, 1863.

A LILY GATHERED.

IN MEMORY OF A LITTLE GIRL.

EAR Mary's home! that Lily sweet
In paradise doth bloom;
She was a flower too passing fair
For this cold vale of gloom.

God needed that bright flow'ret
To gem His garden fair,
So sent and took her to Himself,
To bloom in beauty there.

She, destined for a kindlier soil,
Droop'd, faded, day by day,
Till, on the wings of faith and love,
That lov'd one pass'd away.

Ne'er had she sought the narrow way,
All, all was dark as night,
Until a text, given by a friend,
Turn'd darkness into light.

No more harassing doubts and fears
Distrest that little child,
Her soul was now at peace with God,
By Jesus reconciled.

o 2

All now was perfect peace, yea, joy,
 Jesus had given her rest,
Encircled by His arms, her head
 Lay cradled on His breast.

No sigh, no murmur e'er was heard
 From that sad couch of pain,
Content to live, resigned to die,
 She knew death would be gain.

A lamb of Jesus' blood-bought flock,
 Redeemed by love divine,
She viewed her many sufferings as
 But needed discipline.

Her faith was simple, bright her hope,
 And though she pined away,
She patient was, yea, cheerful, calm,
 For Jesus was her stay.

And when at length God's angel came
 And took her in His arms,
She joyful went to her bright home,
 Death *now* had no alarms.

Her faithful friend and teacher kind,
 Who taught her day by day,
And tended her with so much love,
 Was absent far away.

But ere dear Mary fell asleep,
 She left fond words of love
To that sincere, devoted friend
 Who led her thoughts above.

" Tell her that when she comes to Jesus,
  I will her see," she said,
And with " Glory" on her infant lips,
  Her gentle spirit fled.

And now, in amaranthine bowers,
  ' Neath a more genial sky,
That lily fair in beauty blooms,
  Heaven's crystal waters by.

And 'mid the ransomed choirs of Heaven
  She chants of Jesus' love,
No clouds can ever gloom the sky
  Of that bright home above !

ELLANGOWAN, *August* 5, 1863.

AT HOME.

ESPITE the billows' deafening roar,
A fragile bark has gained the shore,
Its weary tossings now all o'er,
     Safe moor'd, it lies in peace.

Oft darksome, dreary was the night,
Till Jesus came, then all was light,
His presence put all fears to flight,
     Made ev'ry doubting cease.

Swift was its voyage o'er life's sea,
But not from storms was that barque free,
For oft no haven could it see,
     All was so dark and drear.

Till fell the whisper, " It is I,
Oh ! cheer thee, cheer thee, I am nigh,
Now to my loving bosom fly,
     Then gone will be each fear.

" Safe pillow'd on My gentle breast
The weakest lamb may peaceful rest,
Then, little one, be not distrest,
     Till death I will keep thee."

Thus cheer'd, her barque did glide along,
The Cross was still its Anchor strong,
And Jesus was her Hope and Song
      O'er life's unquiet sea.

Wave after wave did o'er her roll,
But Jesus did their rage control,
They did but waft her weary soul
      More swift to " yonder side."

Moor'd to the Rock of Ages sure,
She could all suff'rings calm endure,
They did to Jesus her allure,
      Where she did safely hide.

At length is gained the radiant shore,
Safe is that barque moor'd evermore,
For storms can reach it nevermore!
      All *there* is calm for aye.

Then, dearest sister, dry thy tears,
Soon, soon shall pass life's fleeting years,
E'en now to thee that shore appears,
      It neareth day by day.

Her message left to thee, how sweet!
And when for glory thou art meet,
That lamb will hasten thee to greet
      On Heaven's blissful strand.

May many, many taught by thee,
Be led to Jesus' love to flee,
That thou in glory mayest see
      The labours of thine hand.

A fellow-worker with thy God,
Aye tread the path that Jesus trod,
It leadeth to that bright abode
   Prepared by Him for thee.

And when thy work on earth is o'er,
Thy loved, not lost, *but* gone before,
Shall hail thee on that tranquil shore
   Where is a crystal sea !

ELLANGOWAN, *Sept.* 10, 1863.

ACROSTIC.

TO A FRIEND.

JOY in thy gracious Saviour, He's ever near
to thee,
A nd on His bosom resting, calm, peaceful
must thou be,
N o danger can befall thee, no ill can thee
betide,
E 'en now His eye beams on thee, He's ever at thy
side,
T o strengthen and uphold thee, grace needed He'll
provide.

K eep ever close to Jesus, for He will be thy Stay,
E 'en till thou rest in glory He'll keep thee day by day,
N or will He e'er forsake thee, He'll cease to guide
thee never,
N or from His heart so loving can anything thee sever;
E 'en death cannot divide thee, thou 'lt dwell with Him
for ever,
D well in His blissful presence where joy reigns
evermore,
Y ea, for sorrow's known not on Heaven's peaceful
shore.

October 14, 1863.

TO JEANIE.

NCE more I wish thee joy, Jeanie !
  On this thy natal day,
Another year of cares and toils
  Has pass'd from earth away. .

Another year of privilege,
  Of sunny smiles and tears,
For oft in many a trying scene
  Hath God dispelled thy fears.

Thy circle has unbroken been
  Throughout the bygone year,
What cause for deepest thankfulness,
  And praise, my Jeanie dear.

Yes, you and I have sparèd been
  To hail this day once more,
Whilst many a barque is safely moor'd
  On Canaan's tranquil shore.

Many who bade as fair for life
  This day last year as we,
Are sleeping in the lone churchyard,
  Soon as them we may be.

A few more fleeting years at best,
  And our course will be run,
The sands of life are falling fast,
  Ere long may set life's sun.

Then while 'tis day improve its hours,
  For ah ! they're fleeting fast,
Soon, soon may fall the shades of night,
  Day cannot alway last.

But when in Jesus, all is well,
  'Twill aye be light to thee,
Behind the cloud the sun still shines,
  Which thou by faith may'st see.

Adown the narrow stream of life
  May thy barque smoothly glide,
May no dark storms against it rise
  Till safe on " yonder side."

Bright and unclouded be thy sky,
  May sunshine gild thy way,
With loving friends around thy path,
  Calm glide shall life away.

But ah ! this cannot alway be,
  Sad changes will befall,
Blanks will be made amid our loved—
  Decay is stamped on all.

In sickness as in health, loved one,
  In sorrow as in joy,
'Neath Jesus' shade may'st thou abide,
  Then nought can thee annoy.

A silver lining, Jeanie dear,
   May each cloud have to thee,
Rainbowed with sweetest promises
   May darkling skies aye be.

For, anchor'd on the Rock of Ages,
   Safe is thy fragile bark,
'Twill plough the wild and surging deep
   In light days as in dark.

A New Port thou hast touched this day,
   Soon reached may be the last;
Ere thou anew thy path pursue,
   Pause, and review the past.

Again commit thy way to God,
   Pray Him thy Guide to be,
Until the tossings all are o'er
   Of life's unquiet sea.

Then onward haste, mine own dear friend,
   The port of peace is nearing,
Each wave but wafts thee nearer shore,
   E'en now is land appearing.

And when thy little barque lies moor'd
   On that calm, peaceful shore,
Nor raging waves, nor furious storms,
   Shall vex it evermore!

I fear that sad, most sad, Jeanie,
   Must seem this birthday lay;
But oh! forgive your loving friend,
   It cannot aye be May.

Most precious is thy love to me,
  Friend of mine early day,
My friend in dark days as in bright,
  God bless thee now, alway!

November 8, 1863.

THE DIRGE OF THE OLD YEAR.

TIME is flying,
 I am dying,
Mine hours pass swift away;
 I'll soon be gone
 Up to God's throne,
My record down to lay.

 My locks are white,
 Dim is my sight,
I agèd am and weary;
 My steps are slow,
 My voice is low,
And life is very dreary.

 My tardy feet,
 No longer fleet,
Are by old age encumbered;
 'Tis winter now,
 Cold is my brow,
Life's shivering sands are numbered,

 At midnight drear,
 Which draweth near,
Will my short race be run;
 My funeral knell
 To all will tell
That set is my last sun.

A merry peal
My fate will seal,
'Twill ring in a New Year ;
And I, the old,
In death am cold,
Forgot midst mirth and cheer.

But ah ! take heed,
With lightning speed
I'll mount to yonder throne,
Thine ev'ry thought,
By thee forgot,
Thy ways all to make known.

As midnight chimes,
To brighter climes
I'll wing my weary flight ;
I'll join the past,
O'er me is cast
Oblivion's dark night.

But I'll appear
When death is near,
When earthly visions fade,
A friend I'll be,
To comfort thee
If thou thy peace hast made.

A witness swift,
My voice I'll lift
And hidden things reveal,
Or good or bad,
Or gay or sad,
I nothing shall conceal.

The stranger born,
To-morrow morn,
Hail thou with holy joy ;
His ev'ry hour,
With all thy power,
Thou to God's praise employ.

For weal or woe,
A friend or foe,
On that great day he 'll be,
Then do thou live,
That he may give
A good account of thee.

And now, adieu !
Life's sands are few,
E'en now shall fall the last ;
One moment more—
All now is o'er.
I 've joined the awful past.

Thou Child of Time, thy mission's o'er ;
From earth thou 'rt fled for evermore.
A record sad thou 'lt give to God.
But may our souls in Jesus' blood
Be cleansed anew ; then, from that flood
We 'll come forth spotless, pure as snow,
To tread the desert path of woe.

December 31, 1863.

NEARER HOME.

HOW swift, yet how still, has a year circled
round !
With what joy and what mirth was its
bright morning crowned !
How sweet its rememberings ! now sad and now bright,
Now ' tis gone ! fled away ! as a dream of the night.

For the swift tide of years not a moment stands still,
Till Time is no longer, roll onward it will :
On to Eternity, onward 'twill speed,
Till lost in that ocean, nought its course can impede.

With deep import fraught was the year that has been ;
A nation did hail, with its dearly loved Queen,
Her Son's happy union with Denmark's fair Flower,
May God on them both His best blessings shower.

They have set sail together on life's fitful sea ;
Not vex'd by the storm may their barque ever be ;
May it glide gently on 'neath a bright, cloudless sky ;
Its Pilot be Jesus till moor'd safe on high.

When calm is the sea, as a babe in its sleep,
When the azure sky's bright, not a vigil we keep,
Our little barque floats on its still, glassy breast,
Not a ripple e'er ruffling its deep, tranquil rest.

Not a breeze swells our sails, not a wavelet is seen,
We rest on our oars, all is solemn, serene;
As we gaze on this scene, fain thus would we stay,
Forgetting that sunlight swift fleeteth away.

We dream not of danger, we dread not the night,
Beneath all is calm, and above all is light;
In beauty all's smiling, we see nought to fear,
No rocks and no quicksands, no whirlpools seem near.

But changeful, inconstant, is that silent sea,
We oft seem to stand still, yet this cannot be,
For our barque glides along with the swift-flowing tide,
Which now kisseth the beach, and now rolleth in pride.

Then let us beware of this perilous deep,
Be vigilant, wary, ne'er slumber nor sleep,
For this fair, lovely scene, bathed in peace and in light,
May be changed, ah! how soon, to tempest and night.

Hark! a far distant sound now steals on the ear,
The mariner starts! for it swift draweth near,
'Tis the moan of the wind as it sweeps o'er the deep,
Awaking its waves from their soft, happy sleep.

Now angry and troubled is its erst waveless breast,
The tempest is howling, all is warring, unrest,
The storm-cloud has veilèd that bright summer sky,
The waves are now billows, which run mountains high.

The lightnings now gleam, and the thunders loud crash,
'Gainst each frail little bark the proud billows dash,
No beacon light's seen on that dark cheerless night,
O'er that wild surging sea, not a haven's in sight.

Dost thou see yon light barque drifting on with the tide,
With no anchor, no compass, no pilot to guide?
Can it weather the storm? no, nought can it save—
It is lost, 'tis engulphed by the deep yawning wave.

It is thus with the soul on pleasure's smooth sea—
It sees not its dangers, from its rocks does not flee;
Unconscious, it drifts with that treacherous tide,
Thus asleep, it will ne'er see the bright " yonder side."

It has lived without God in the calm sunny day,
And now in the dark night, that God's far away,
It awakes! looks around! not a Refuge is nigh,
It has slept, ah! *too* long—it awakes but to die.

But can yon tiny barque this dread tempest outride?
Ah! yes, it is safe whatsoe'er may betide,
Though the foam-crested waves do make it their sport,
It will still onward speed till it reaches the port.

'Tis thus with the Christian on life's fretful sea,
His barque glides securely, ne'er lost can it be,
Through tempest and tossing it safe does abide,
For sure is its Anchor and skilful its Guide.

The Cross is that Anchor, its Pilot the Lord,
The Breeze is God's Spirit, its Compass His Word;
The mariner fears not, he smiles at the storm,
For it doth but the will of his Father perform.

His Anchor is Hope, within the veil cast
On the sure Rock of Ages, Love holdeth it fast,
'Tis linked by a chain to the bright throne above,
A chain of enduring, unchanging, deep love.

Though the waves, then, of sorrow around him may roll,
There is One in that barque who their rage can control,
In that dark hour he flees to Jesus' fond breast,
Who but " Peace, be still," whispers, and all is at rest.

Brave, then, onward he steers, though the fierce waters
    roar,
Each billow, hope-crested, but wafts him to shore,
Which by faith he now views, though wild waves roll
    between,
E'en its peace is now felt 'mid the dreariest scene.

We have reached a New Port, and it may be the last,
To many it will be, for ere this year's past
Their barque shall lie anchor'd on that radiant shore,
Where winds and where waves rise and rage nevermore!

Many a barque has been launched in the year now
    gone by,
Whilst many have gained the bright Haven on high,
E'en now some are toiling o'er that stormy deep,
Far distant from land, alas ! too many sleep.

Then on ! Christian Mariner, this day start anew
O'er life's faithless sea, brave, thy voyage pursue,
Oh ! faint not, nor fear, though the storm o'er thee sweeps,
The Golden Strand neareth ! and *Jesus* thee keeps !

    January 1, 1864.

NEW YEAR'S HYMN FOR CHILDREN.

DOST thou see that willow weeping
O'er that little, lonely grave?
Jesus o'er it watch is keeping,
One sleeps there He died to save.

This day last year she was praising,
Singing of her Saviour's love,
Now she's hallelujahs raising
In her happy home above.

She had, in her life's bright morning,
Come to Jesus and found rest,
He, that little lamb not scorning,
Kept her cradled in His breast.

She little thought last New Year's meeting,
As she sung her New Year's song,
That ere another New Year's greeting
She'd have joined the ransom'd throng.

" Time is short," and life is fleeting !
But eternity, how long !
Oh ! may we, in glory meeting,
Sing with her the sweet New Song.

Let us, then, improve each warning,
  Give to God our youthful day,
For, ere another New Year's morning,
  We, too, may have pass'd away.

January 1, 1864.

TO LIZZIE.

INE own little Lizzie, my sunbeam so
bright,
My star to illumine life's dark, dreary
night,
Many happy returns of this day mayst thou see,
A bright Summer's day may this life be to thee.

May thy sky ne'er be darkling, thy pathway ne'er drear,
It cannot be lonely with the best of friends near,
May roses and lilies around thy steps twine,
And if it be good for thee, the sunshine be thine.

But should a cloud float athwart thy' bright sky,
Then look thou to Jesus, the Friend ever nigh,
Then thy path through this valley be it ever so weary,
With Him as thy Solace, can never be dreary.

As the oak and the ivy is thy heart and mine,
As closely united as the branch and the vine,
Whose tendrils entwined, the one with the other,
So fond and so clinging that 'twere death them to sever.

Eighteen bright happy summers have pass'd o'er thy head,
And thou through them all hast in safety been led,
On Faith and Hope's pinions mount ever and soar,
Till thou drop them at Heaven's gate, to need them no
more.

They are needed not *there*, for *there* all is light,
And Hope is fruition, and Faith there is sight,
'Tis Love that will reign there, for Jesus is Love,
And He is the Light of that bright land above.

Oh ! seek Him then *now* in thy summer-time bright,
And ne'er will He leave thee should fall a dark night ;
Should sorrows distress thee, or tears dim thine eye,
Oh ! fear not, in that hour is Jesus most nigh.

All dark is the future, not a step can we see,
But 'tis better, far better for thee and for me,
In the hands of our God we would leave all our cares,
All our tears, all our fears, all our sorrows He shares.

And now, mine own darling, methinks thou wilt say,
" What a sermon is this on my glad natal day !
What a shame of Mamma to lecture me so,
That I do not like it, I am sure she must know."

But, forgive thy fond mother, fain, fain would she see
Her loved ones in Jesus, then happy she'd be ;
Oh ! to meet all in glory, to part nevermore,
All the tears and the fears of this weary life o'er.

To taste of the pleasures at our Father's right hand,
To spend endless years in that bright happy land,
To bask in its bowers, with melody rife,
To repose 'neath the shade of the sweet Tree of Life.

That thus it may be is thy mother's fond prayer,
For, oh ! it were sad were our loved ones not there ;
We are now one on earth, may we be one in Heaven,
Where friendships are lasting, where ties are ne'er riven.

To the love of our God I now thee commend,
May He bless thee and keep thee, be ever thy Friend,
May He give thee *His* peace, which the world may not
  know,
Then a sunbeam thou 'lt be whereso'er thou mayst go.

January 13, 1864.

344

IN MEMORY OF A BELOVED AUNT.

OBT. 18TH JANUARY 1864.

THOU art gone to thy rest—we would not
　　recall thee ;
　　Ah ! no, for thy sufferings are o'er ;
　　In the home of the blest no ill can befall
　　　thee—
With Jesus thou 'lt dwell evermore.

Thou art gone to thy rest—on the bosom of Love
　　Thy spirit in rapture 's reclining,
All is light, all is joy in that bright land above,
　　There the Sun is eternally shining.

Thou art gone to thy rest—thy pathway to glory
　　Was through tribulation and pain ;
Long, long years of sickness completed life's story,
　　But our loss was thine infinite gain.

Thou art gone to thy rest—oft, oft wast thou weary,
　　For sufferings many were thine ;
But aye cheerful thou wast, though thy path was so
　　　dreary,
　　Thy countenance peaceful, benign.

Thou art gone to thy rest—at death's hour to uphold
thee
Thy trusted, loved Saviour was nigh,
To cheer thy faint heart, in His arms to enfold thee, .
And softly to whisper, "'Tis I."

Thou art gone to thy rest—thy loved boys would greet
thee,
Whose loss thou didst so long deplore,
They would haste to the portals of glory to meet thee—
Ye have met—ye shall part nevermore.

Thou art gone to thy rest—in Jesus thou 'rt sleeping,
How calm and how peaceful that sleep !
O'er thy lone narrow bed watch angels are keeping ;
Thou 'lt wake not from that sleep to weep.

Thou art gone to thy rest—the tear may be shed,
But ah ! 'tis of joy, not of sorrow,
For from pain, and from grief, and from sin thou hast
fled,
No fear of death brings Heaven's morrow.

Thou art gone to thy rest—thy warm welcome we miss,
Thy husband is weary and lone,
But a short little while and he 'll join thee in bliss,
To worship before the bright throne.

Thou art gone to thy rest—a fond mother wert thou,
A wife, ever dutiful, kind ;
Thy heart was so tender, so placid thy brow,
Thou wast in the furnace refined.

Thou art gone to thy rest—the tear-drop is falling,
  To think that thou wert all alone,
When the Angel of Death was heard on thee calling,
  When Jesus thee claimed as His own.

Thou art gone to thy rest—but no loved one was near
  To wipe the death-dew from thy brow,
To catch thy fond smile, and thy last words to hear,
  For longing to go home wert thou.

Thou art gone to thy rest—to this dark vale of earth
  We would not recall thee, ah ! no;
For the day of thy death was the day of thy birth
  To joys which we *now* may not know.

Thou art gone to thy rest—then let us not weep,
  That ended is life with its woes ;
But as calm and as peaceful may we go to sleep,
  For sweet is the Christian's repose !

Thou art gone to thy rest—'mid the glories of Heaven
  Thy deep tide of joy ever flows,
Life's trials all o'er, and thy sins all forgiven,
  Thy soul with ecstatic bliss glows.

Thou art gone to thy rest—*but* a few fleeting years,
  And we'll join thee, ne'ermore to part ;
But to spend endless years, wiped away all our tears,
  One in love, one in joy, one in heart !

  February 15, 1864.

PRAYER AND PROMISE.

 H, Jesus ! Thou who art " *The Way*,"
Thee let me follow day by day,
Till, guided by Thy hand of love,
I rest me in the fold above.

" I am the Way," oh ! walk with Me,
And foes shall ne'er come nigh to thee,
I'll lead thee to the joys above,
Where ev'ry heart's replete with love.

Oh, Jesus ! Thou who art " *The Truth*,"
Be Thou the Teacher of our youth,
Lord, I believe, Thy words abide,
Then, 'neath Thy wing, oh ! let me hide.

" I am the Truth," oh ! trust in Me,
Believe and live, ne'er faithless be,
My promises to thee are sure,
Firm as a rock shall they endure.

Oh, Jesus ! Thou who art " *The Life*,"
I'll dwell in Thee, secure from strife,
At death, through Thee, to life I'll soar,
A life that dure shall evermore.

" I am the Life," oh ! cling to Me,
As vine and branch so let us be,
'Tis only thus that thou canst live,
Abide in Me, strength I'll thee give.

Oh, Jesus ! Thou who art " *The Light*,"
Make this dark vale of gloom all bright ;
A pillar be, of cloud by day,
Of fire by night, to point the way.

" I am the Light," oh ! look to Me,
Then night can ne'er o'ershadow thee,
Thou shalt a child be of the day,
Ne'er, ne'er shall darkness gloom thy way.

Oh, Jesus ! Thou who art " *The Rock*,"
Ne'er let me dread the tempest's shock,
Hid in its clift, secure am I,
Each crested wave me passes by.

" I am the Rock," oh ! cleave to Me,
'Mid raging waves I will keep thee,
Unmovèd, storms may o'er thee roll,
Thou 'lt smile, for calm shall be thy soul.

Oh, Jesus ! Thou who art " *The Rest*,"
Be Thou my Joy when sore opprest,
My pillow Thy fond bosom be,
Now, and through all eternity !

" I am the Rest," oh ! lean on Me,
All through life's day I 'll solace thee.
And My fond, gentle, loving breast,
Shall be through endless years thy Rest !

March 19, 1864.

TO TOM.

NCE more I hail, mine own dear boy, thy
    happy natal day,
    Another year has swiftly past, Time speedeth
    fast away;
Oh ! then, improve its golden hours, whilst health and
    strength are thine,
To seek thy God and heavenly things thy youthful
    heart incline.

Come to the loving Saviour *now*, and He will give thee
    rest,
And when by doubts and fears assailed, flee to His
    gentle breast ;
Him love and serve with all thine heart, and He will be
    thy Friend.
In all thy ways He'll counsel thee, success shall thee
    attend.

May sunshine gild thine onward path, if it be good for
    thee,
And for the blessings of thy lot, O deeply grateful be !
Walk humbly with thy gracious God when all is calm
    and bright,
And to His will be thou resigned when falls a
    darksome night.

For ah ! it cannot aye be light, dark clouds *will* gloom
  thy sky,
Dark shadows round thy pathway fall, presaging storms
  are nigh ;
But calm, amid the darkling gloom, thine heart no fear
  shall know,
For trusting in the Lord, thou 'lt say, " My God hath
  willed it so."

This world hath many a snare, my boy, to lead thy soul
  from God :
The path of pleasure flowery is, exceeding smooth and
  broad ;
The path of duty ever keep, how rough soe'er it be,
The happiest and the safest 'twill alway prove to thee.

Temptations oft may thee assail amid the cares of life,
In Jesus' strength them all resist, and conquer in the
  strife ;
For many are the Christian's foes, who oft his faith
  will try,
But if in Jesus, safe art thou, thou wilt them all defy.

In doing good ne'er weary be, diffuse love, peace, and
  joy,
And to advance thy Saviour's cause thy talents all
  employ ;
In Jesus' footsteps daily tread—a useful life be thine,
So shall His presence go with thee, His love shall on
  thee shine.

A comfort to thy many friends, oh! may'st thou
   alway be,
An honour to thy fellow-men, thy God shall prosper
   thee ;
And in thy home, around our hearth, still be as thou
   hast been—
A loving Son, a Brother kind, enlivening each dark
   scene.

I love to hear in afternoons thy footfall on the stair,
Thou hastenest to thy Mother's room to greet thy loved
   ones there ;
To see thee there we happy are, we gladly welcome
   thee—
The labours of the day oft o'er, a pleasant chat have we.

Home pleasures are the sweetest, best, may they prove
   so to thee,
Thine evenings with us thou dost spend, long, long,
   may thus it be ;
Around thy Mother's cheerful fire, with thy two sisters
   kind,
On many a dreary winter night mayst thou enjoyment
   find.

Thy Mother loves to see you all around her day by day,
Your going out and coming in doth cheer her lonely way ;
Ye gentle are and kind to her—sad, sad her heart
   would be,
But for your loving words and ways, she'd many a dark
   day see.

It makes her heart right glad, my boy, to see thee fond
  of home ;
A blessing thou shalt be to her in all the time to come.
And when our days on earth are o'er, oh ! may we meet
  in Heaven,
For in that bright, that better land, no tender ties are
  riven !

April 17, 1864.

LINES WRITTEN FOR LIZZIE'S ALBUM.

THE VIOLET.

WHILST roaming in a lovely glen, one
sunlit summer's morn,
Admiring all the beauties rare which
did that vale adorn,
I spied a blue-eyed violet, of meek and modest mien,
Which grew upon a mossy bank, close by a crystal
stream ;
Attracted by its artless grace, I staid me on the spot,
Methought it pleading looked at me, and said, " O ! cull
me not,
I'd rather bloom ánd blossom here, in quietude and
shade,
Than deck the gay and gaudy bower where flaunting
beauties fade.
Then leave me here, in sweet content, to live my little day,
And when that little day is o'er, to gently pass away."
Fain, fain would I have culled that flower, to me
surpassing fair,
And ta'en it to adorn my home, to reign in beauty
there.
" I will not cull thee, flow'ret fair, how dear soe'er
thou be,
Still grace thy beauteous valley-home, aye full of childish
glee ;

Bloom on, sweet child of Nature, with modest eye of
blue,
Nursed by the mild and sunny ray, and by the evening
dew."
It gazed at me so witchingly, so trustful was its smile,
That I left it in its beauty, to bloom its little while.
I'd rather have that winsome flower than all the roses
gay,
That rear their proud and stately heads their beauties to
display.

May 16, 1864.

TO MARY.

HOW silently, my Mary dear,
Has pass'd another fleeting year !
Time, with unceasing wing, speeds on,
Soon will its golden hours be gone.

Again has dawned the first of June,
When Nature's clad in glowing bloom,
That day when thou to me wert given,
To cheer my heart with anguish riven.

Thou hast fulfilled a daughter's part,
Thou gladdened hast my bleeding heart,
For many a lonely hour I'd see
Wert thou not near to solace me.

The year now past has darksome been,
Too many sunless days thou'st seen,
Would that it had been otherwise,
That sunny, bright had been thy skies.

May this New Year more lightsome be,
No dark days may it have for thee ;
Though ofttimes they may cloudy prove,
O ! rest assured, all is in love.

A comfort great art thou to me,
My griefs have lightened been by thee ;
So loving and so kind art thou,
A frown ne'er clouds thy sunny brow.

The future is unknown to thee,
But may it happy, brightsome be ;
Be thine a sunny after-life,
All free from envy, care, or strife.

Trust in the Lord, He cares for thee,
In all thy ways thee keep will He ;
Not darkest storms shall e'er thee move—
God will to thee a Refuge prove.

A sunbeam be, my Mary dear,
Thy Mother's lonely heart to cheer ;
For oh ! how sad I oft would be
But for thy loving ways with me.

May God upon thee ever smile,
May sunshine gild life's " little while,"
May thy home be a home of love,
May God its Guardian ever prove.

And when the desert is o'erpast,
When all its toils are o'er at last,
Oh ! may we meet on yon calm shore,
To be with Jesus evermore !

May God's best blessing on thee rest,
May peace and joy now fill thy breast ;
God smile on thee this happy day,
Watch o'er and keep thee now, alway.

And now, my child, I thee commend
To God, thy Hiding-place and Friend;
Nought from *His* love can e'er thee sever,
None from *His* hand can pluck thee ever!

June 1, 1864.

ACROSTIC.

TO A FRIEND.

 AY Jesus bless thee day by day,
A nd may His peace be thine alway,
R est in His love, He cares for thee,
Y ea, e'en till death thee keep will He.

B right be thy path to Heaven above,
R ejoicing in thy Saviour's love,
O h ! trust in Him, He 'll fail thee never,
W hen cloudlets gloom He 'll cheer thee ever,
N ought from His love can e'er thee sever !

A mid the chequered scenes of life
R epose in Him, secure from strife,
R adiant with Hope is now thy sky,
A nd Faith descries its home on high,
N or fears the tempest passing by.

ARRAN, *June* 20, 1864.

ACROSTIC.

TO A YOUNG FRIEND.

J OYOUS and happy mayst thou be,
O h, may God keep thee ever !
H e loves the little ones to bless,
N or will He leave thee ever !

H e 'll be thy Guardian and thy Guide,
E 'en now He 'll lead thee ever !
N ow if thou wilt Him love and serve,
R est shalt thou in His arms of love,
Y ea, sad thou shalt be never !

T hine be a gladsome, useful life,
O h, live to Jesus ever !
W hen foes are nigh, flee to His breast,
N ought there shall harm thee ever !
L ife then shall be a sunny day,
E ach hour shall calmly glide away,
Y ea, dark it can be never !

July 16, 1864.

HOME.

 SEAT me at the window, and I gaze upon the
 sea ;
I love to mark its ebb and flow, to list its
 melody ;

Now is its bosom heaving, all is tossing and unrest,
Now 'tis in peace reposing, as babe on mother's breast.

And seated there I love to gaze across that fitful sea,
Upon the beauteous other side, so very dear to me.

There is my home, with all its loves, though it I may
 not see,
I know 'tis there, though mists of earth do hide that
 home from me.

And yet I cannot reach that home, though now it seems
 so nigh,
'Tis only seen through darkling clouds with Faith's
 keen eagle eye ;

For cross'd must be that stormy deep ere reach'd is
 yonder side ;
But trusting in my Saviour's power, no danger can betide.

And as I muse at twilight hour, when all is calm, serene,
When stillness reigns above, around, when not a cloudlet's
seen,

I think of that bright, holy home, ofttimes so dimly seen,
For do not clouds between my soul and it oft intervene?

But, ah! the Sun breaks forth, He comes! doubtings
and fears all flee,
I see that glorious Home of homes prepared by Love
for me.

Yet pass'd must be the Jordan flood ere I can reach that
shore,
And meet again those cherish'd ones,—not lost, but
gone before.

But circled in the arms of love, I'll fear not death's dark
wave,
It shall not overflow my soul, for *Jesus* will me save.

He'll sweetly whisper in that hour, " Fear not, my
child, I'm nigh,
I'll bear thee through the swelling tide, safe to thy home
on high."

BURNTISLAND, *August* 22, 1864.

ACROSTIC.

JOYOUS and bright be life's young Spring,
O h ! be it blighted never !
H ope on ! a useful life be thine,
N or darksome be it ever !

E 'en though a cloudlet veil thy sky,
D ream not 'twill last for ever !
M ay Jesus' love disperse the gloom,
O h ! then, afraid be never.
N e'er will He leave thee, He is nigh,
D aily He 'll keep thee ever !

M ay many sunny years be thine !
I mprove life's bright hours ever.
D ay after day it passeth swift,
D ark, lonesome be it never !
L ist to the gentle voice of Love,
" E 'en *now* trust in Me ever !
T hy youthful heart, oh ! give to Me ;
O n Me repose, I will keep thee,
N ow, henceforth, and for ever !"

BURNTISLAND, *Sept.* 19, 1864.

STANZA.

ONE by one are friends departing
 To the blissful land of rest ;
Now on Jesus' bosom leaning,
 They are holy, they are blest.
Sorrow there can ne'er distress them—
 They have wept their latest tear,
Nor temptations e'er molest them—
 They have felt their latest fear.

With the angels and the saintèd
 They are hymning Jesus' love ;
'Neath His smile they now are basking
 In that happy Land above.
Soon, it may be, we may join them,
 Chant with them of love divine ;
Ransomed by the blood of Jesus,
 They now in His likeness shine.

October 23, 1864.

TO JEANIE.

ND now another year, Jeanie, has fled
from earth away,
And I am once more privileged to hail thy
natal day.

Another sunny year, Jeanie, has passèd o'er thy head,
Whilst many a one, healthful as thou, are number'd with
the dead.

Then ever grateful be, Jeanie, for good is God to thee,
His hand hath led thee on till now, and still thy Guide
He'll be.

Oh ! walk with Him in love, Jeanie, and keep the narrow
way,
And like unto a little child He'll lead thee day by day.

And shouldst thou weary be, Jeanie, He'll fold thee to
His breast ;
Safe nestling there, thy fainting soul in perfect peace may
rest.

All through this dreary vale, Jeanie, thy Sun and Shield
He'll be,
Nor darksome night, nor angry foe, shall e'er come
nigh to thee.

Should dark clouds gloom thy sky, Jeanie, oh, faint
    not, do not fear !
No clouds can hide the Christian's Sun, ah ! no, He's
    ever near.

Then with Faith's eagle eye, Jeanie, pierce through the
    darkest night,
And see unveiled thy Saviour's face, for where He is, is
    light.

His smile is Heaven's light, Jeanie, *His* presence endless
    joy ;
Then cheer thee, since He's ever near, nought can thy
    peace destroy.

To all His own dear ones, Jeanie, He gives His own
    deep peace,
Then rest in Him, that so thy joy may more and more
    increase.

And when life's cheerless day, Jeanie, is drawing to a
    close,
On Jesus' loving bosom still thy weary head repose.

He'll bear thee in His arms, Jeanie, through Jordan's
    swelling tide,
It shall not overflow thy soul, thou 'lt reach the yonder
    side.

There loving friends shall greet thee, Jeanie—ye 'll meet
    no more to sever ;
No sad adieus, no parting tears, on that calm shore for
    ever.

And now on this bright day, Jeanie, to God I thee
commend,
All good things may He give to thee, mine own, mine
early friend.

Friend in the storm and calm, Jeanie, in dark days as in
bright,
How oft hast thou illumed and cheered my life's sad,
dreary night!

A loving, faithful friend, Jeanie, hast thou been aye
to me,
Then to each other fond and true, oh! may we alway be.

Cheering each other on, Jeanie, along life's pathway
drear,
And with the gentle hand of love a-wiping off each tear.

Strengthening each other's hands, Jeanie, soothing each
other's heart,
In days of sickness and of grief, solace to each impart.

Our friendship formed on earth, Jeanie, shall bloom
again in Heaven,
For *there* the sacred ties of love shall nevermore be riven.

How sweet is then the thought, Jeanie, that nought
shall e'er us sever,
But with our Jesus and loved ones we'll rest and reign
for ever!

November 8, 1864.

FOUND.

WAS a little weary child,
Wand'ring about the street,
When this day last year as I wept,
A soft voice did me greet,

"Why weepest thou, my little one?
Art thou alone and cold?"
My tears fell fast, I could not speak—
My little tale was told.

She took me gently by the hand,
Spoke kindly unto me,
And brought me to this happy fold,
Where I now love to be.

Here first I heard of Jesus' love
To wand'ring lambs like me,
That if I would but come to Him,
He would my Saviour be.

That He would all my sins forgive,
For He had died for me,
And that He loves the lambs to bless—
Their Shepherd kind is He.

Grace touch'd my heart, a weary lamb
  To Him came seeking rest,
He welcom'd me, and bade me lie
  Safe folded to His breast.

And now I am His little lamb,
  I feel my sins forgiven,
That He'll be with me all through life,
  Then welcome me to Heaven.

My daily wants hath He supplied
  Throughout the year now past,
A trustful, grateful heart be mine—
  On Him all cares I cast.

God bless the faithful, loving friend
  Who kindly led me here,
And may we sing of Jesus' love
  Through Heaven's eternal Year.

December 25, 1864.

THE LAST WORDS OF THE DYING YEAR.

UT a few more moments and I shall pass
Into the silent Land, to return no more.
To join my brethren of the past I wing
My flight up to God's throne, there to give in
A faithful record ; then shall I sleep till
The last trump shall sound, when awake I shall
To meet again frail man, ah ! not now frail,
But clad in robes of immortality,
Ne'ermore to taste the bitter cup of death.
With shouts of deepest joy shall some me welcome
On that day, because of sweet rememberings
Recalled by me ; days spent in deeds of good ;
Hours pass'd in commune with his Saviour-God ;
Whilst some—alas ! *too* many—shrink affrighted will
From my piercing glance, and seek to hide them
From the dread sight of God; it cannot be—
They must confront me, and from the great Judge
Himself hear the sad words, " Depart from Me."
Then think, O man, while lasts the day of grace,
How short is Time ; improve its precious hours,
And give thyself to God, e'en *Now*, this night,
Ere I depart, that I may tell the tale
To listening angels, who will joy o'er thee ;
Then come, O come, e'en *Now*, for Jesus waits
To welcome thee, and give thee His own peace.

Mine infant brother, born as I expire,
Welcomed by some with praise, with mirth by some,
Oh ! use him well, in thy God's service spend
His golden moments, that he may witness
A good account of thee.   And now I go ;
My sands are well-nigh run, my short race o'er ;
Oh ! list my latest words, work, watch, and pray ;
Dear friends, " Adieu !" one moment more, I 'm gone !

December 31, 1864.

TIME'S MESSAGE.

" He which testifieth these things, saith, ' Surely I come quickly ;'
Amen ! Even so come, Lord Jesus."

PASSING is *Time* away,
　Years wax and wane,
Golden hours, once gone by,
　Come not again.
Treasure it as you may,
Passing is *Time* away—
　Passing away !

Passing is *Grace* away,
　Seek God *to-day;*
Now 's the accepted time,
　Oh ! why delay ?
Jesus' kind voice obey ;
Passing is *Grace* away—
　Passing away !

Passing is *Day* away,
　Night draweth nigh ;
And as the tree falleth,
　So shall it lie.
As the sun's flitting ray,
Passing is *Day* away—
　Passing away !

Passing are *Years* away !
Gone evermore !
That Year of endless years
Wanes nevermore !
Last shall its spring-time aye,
Passing are *Years* away—
Passing away !

Passing is *Health* away,
Heart and strength fail ;
Death culls the fairest flowers,
Brighest cheeks pale.
All are to pain a prey,
Passing is *Health* away—
Passing away !

Passing is *Wealth* away,
E'en as 'tis sought ;
God, and not mammon, love—
He changeth not.
Earth's treasures swift decay,
Passing is *Wealth* away—
Passing away !

Passing are *Joys* away,
Scarce worth a thought ;
All below's vanity,
With sorrow fraught.
Pleasure oft lures astray,
Passing are *Joys* away—
Passing away !

Passing is *War* away,
  Discord shall cease ;
Throughout the nations all
  There shall be peace.
Stay'd be the deadly fray ;
Passing is *War* away—
  Passing away !

Passing is *Life* away,
  On ! Pilgrim, on !
Soon will the goal be reach'd !
  Soon the crown won !
Linger not by the way,
Passing is *Life* away—
  Passing away !

Passing is *Pain* away,
  Cheer, suff'rer, cheer,
Thy couch of languishing
  Sees Jesus near ;
All thy pangs He'll allay,
Passing is *Pain* away—
  Passing away !

Passing are *Friends* away,
  Gone to their rest,
Into the Heav'nly Land,
  Home of the Blest.
From this frail house of clay
Passing are *Friends* away—
  Passing away !

Passing is *Grief* away,
  Though shadows pall ;
In the bright Evermore
  Tears may not fall.
There sorrow may not stay,
Passing is *Grief* away—
  Passing away !

Passing is *Gloom* away,
  Dark clouds of fear,
Touch'd by Love's gentle hand,
  Swift disappear.
'Neath Jesus' cheering ray
Passing is *Gloom* away—
  Passing away !

Passing is *Faith* away,
  Soon 'twill be sight,
Hope full fruition be,
  Love endless light ;
That may reign endless day,
Passing is *Faith* away—
  Passing away !

Passing is *Prayer* away,
  Needed no more ;
Round the all-glorious throne
  Wrestling is o'er ;
There all is Song for aye,
Passing is *Prayer* away—
  Passing away !

Passing is *Sin* away,
  Oh ! happy thought ;
Into the Holy Land
  Sin enters not.
Dawn heralds perfect day,
Passing is *Sin* away—
  Passing away !

Passing is *Night* away,
  Soon will day break ;
Faint streaks of light appear,
  Sleeper awake !
Up ! arise ! watch and pray,
Passing is *Night* away—
  Passing away !

Passing is *Death* away,
  Why, mourner, weep ?
They who in Jesus live,
  They in Him sleep.
Safe in His love are they ;
Passing is *Death* away—
  Passing away !

January 1, 1865.

NEW YEAR'S HYMN FOR CHILDREN.

HE time is short! a Year has fled,
    Since we last hail'd this day,
And with it many a cherish'd friend
    From earth has pass'd away.

And we, too, ere this New Year close,
    May fade, and droop, and die;
Then let us day by day prepare
    For our bright Home on high.

We bless thee, Jesus, for Thy love,
    To us so freely given,
We now would give our hearts to Thee,
    Oh! make us heirs of Heaven.

Our many sins, O Lord, forgive,
    And keep us lest we stray;
This New-born Year is dark to us,
    Oh! lead us day by day.

From grace to glory may we haste,
    Cheer'd onward by Thy smile;
Be Thou our Guardian and our Guide
    Through all life's " little while."

And when our last New Year is o'er,
May we—a happy band—
All meet, to hail a bright New Year,
Safe in the Better Land!

January 1, 1865.

TO LIZZIE.

ANOTHER year is gone, my child; hath
it not fleeted fast?
Reminding us that youth and health will
not for ever last;
For Summer swift succeeds to Spring, with all its
flow'rets gay,
But only for a while they bloom—they, too, shall fade
away.

Then Autumn comes, with changeful skies, with sere
and yellow leaf,
The flow'rets fade, the days decline, proclaiming life is
brief!
Then Winter crowns the dying year, so bleak, so chill,
so drear;
Yet doth the Christian's eagle eye see budding Spring-
time near.

Then may thy Spring-time, Lizzie dear, put forth its
blossoms fair,
Nor fear though dark clouds gloom thy sky, though
cold winds chill the air;
For Spring is oft a changeful scene, now sunshine and
now shower,
But, ah! 'tis this that nourishes, that beautifies the flower.

Then shall thy life's young Summer be all beauteous
    and all bright,
No chilling blast shall mar its bloom, nor withering
    wind it blight;
The noon-day sun, the evening dew, its beauty shall in-
    crease,
Till mellow Autumn comes at length, an eve of calm
    and peace.

A harvest rich, mine own loved one, may it then yield
    to thee,
O! may the seed sown in youth's Spring, with joy then
    gathered be,
That when bleak Winter-tide sets in, with long and
    dreary nights,
It may to thee a season be of holy, calm delights.

O! be the snows of age to thee a crown of holy joy,
Beloved by all thy many friends, may nought thy peace
    destroy;
Strong in thy Saviour's strength, thou'lt brave the
    fiercest storms of life,
Assured that in the end thou'lt be a victor in the strife.

And when thy reign on earth is o'er, then shall the
    reaper, Death,
Thee take from this cold winter world, a flower of
    heavenly birth,
To bloom in a more genial clime, where skies are all
    serene,
Whose Spring-time reigns for evermore, where meads
    are ever green.

There blooms the beauteous Tree of Life, whose boughs
    shall shade thee ever !
There flow'rets amaranthine bloom, there flows life's
    crystal river ;
Nor scorching sun, nor chilling blast shall beat upon
    thee ever !
In holy beauty thou shalt grow—thy bloom shall fade,
    ah ! never !

That I may meet thee, dear loved child, in Eden's vernal
    bowers,
And with our loving Saviour bloom with all His gather'd
    flowers,
Him follow wheresoe'er He leads, ne'ermore to know
    decay,
Is thine own mother's earnest prayer on this thy natal
    day.

January 13, 1865.

ACROSTIC.

TO A FRIEND.

 AY Jesus bless thee day by day,
A nd may He sun thy pilgrim way!
R est in the Lord, He cares for thee,
G uide, Guardian, Friend to thee He 'll
be.
A mid the din and cares of life,
R epose in Him, secure from strife;
E 'en till thou reach thy Home above,
T rust in His deathless, changeless love.

P ursue thy journey 'neath His wing,
R ound thee His loving arms He 'll fling,
E 'en *His* own peace He 'll give to thee,
T ill life is o'er thee keep will He.
S trong in His strength, go on thy way,
E re long 'twill end in Glory's Day:
L et nought from Jesus e'er thee sever—
L ean on His gentle bosom ever!

February 23, 1865.

A BIRTH-DAY WISH.

H ! wilt Thou keep me, precious Saviour !
    Through all life's changing year,
    In health and sickness, joy and grief,
    Oh ! wilt Thou aye be near ?

Yes, I will keep thee, little one,
    Through all life's fleeting day,
And when shall fall the shades of eve,
    I 'll be thy Strength and Stay.

Oh ! wilt Thou keep me, precious Saviour !
    Whene'er I go astray,
And wander in the paths of sin,
    Wilt Thou me lead each day ?

Yes, I will keep thee, feeble one,
    E'en though thou shouldest stray,
I 'll follow thee, and bring thee back
    Into the narrow way.

Oh ! wilt Thou keep me, gentle Jesus !
    When all around is night ?
Oh ! will Thy hand wipe off the tear,
    And make the darkness light ?

Yes, I will keep thee, mourning one,
  Come unto *Me* and rest,
I'll bear thee in Mine arms of love,
  I'll fold thee to My breast.

Oh! wilt Thou keep me, precious Jesus!
  In each dark, trying hour,
And keep me from the tempter's wiles
  Safe by Thy mighty power?

Yes, I will keep thee, tempted one,
  When Satan tries thee sore,
Repair to Me, I'll succour thee—
  Cling to Me evermore.

Oh! wilt Thou keep me, precious Saviour!
  When heart and flesh shall fail,
Wilt Thou sustain my fainting heart,
  When passing death's dark vale?

Yes, I will keep thee, dying one,
  When comes the hour of death,
I'll bear thee safe through Jordan's flood,
  And watch thy latest breath.

Oh! wilt Thou keep me, loving Jesus!
  When I in glory rest,
And wander 'mid the bowers of Heaven,
  All happy and all blest?

Yes, I will keep thee, ransomed one,
  Thou shalt My glory see,
And through Heaven's bright, eternal day,
  E'en then I will keep thee.

March 19, 1865.

TO THE PRIMROSE.

HEN I see thee ope thine eye,
Thou dost whisper, "Spring is nigh,"
Dreary Winter's on the wane,
Long and darksome 's been its reign.

Trees and flowers again shall bloom,
Waking from their wintry tomb,
Harbinger of them art thou,
With thy pale, thy pensive brow.

Thou dost herald in the Spring,
Winter's snows are on the wing,
For thou art a fragile child,
Shrinking from the tempest wild.

Hope revives within this heart,
Balm to it thou dost impart,
For if Jesus cares for thee,
Much more will He care for me.

Yes ! He 'll cheer this bleeding heart,
Groaning 'neath affliction's smart,
If I only in Him rest,
Peace shall fill this aching breast.

R

Lowly flow'ret of the vale,
Ne'ermore shall my faint heart fail,
I will, as I gaze on thee,
Think the same Eye keepeth me.

Brighter days are drawing near,
Each sad, mournful heart to cheer,
Nature shall in joyful lays
Chant its great Creator's praise.

Beauty cometh with the Spring,
Woods and vales with mirth shall sing,
Blow, then, gentle flow'ret, blow,
Gone will soon be frosts and snow.

April 3, 1865.

TO TOM.

 NOTHER year, mine own dear boy,
   Has swiftly pass'd away,
And I am once more privileged
   To hail thy natal day.

Thou art of age this festal morn,
   A long, bright life be thine,
And may the Sun of Righteousness
   On all thy pathway shine.

Yet dark clouds may their shadows fling,
   And veil the brightest skies ;
But ah ! e'en in the darkest night
   Hope's bright star will arise.

'Twill point thee to a happier land,
   A land of perfect light—
A land of love and holiness,
   A land that knows no night.

O ! may a rainbow bright, my boy,
   Arch o'er the blackest sky,
The pledge of thy God's faithfulness,
   Soft whisp'ring, " It is I."

'Then steadfast on it keep thine eye,
　Think what's *behind* the cloud,
Thy Sun is alway shining there,
　No gloom can *Him* enshroud.

Earth's joys fade past, mine own dear boy,
　They're but a fleeting dream;
We fain would grasp them, but they're gone,
　As snow-flake on the stream.

Then set thine heart on joys above,
　Which ne'er shall know decay;
For ah! the joys that Jesus gives
　Shall never pass away.

'Then give to God thy manhood's prime,
　And thou shalt happy be,
He'll fill thy cup with all good things—
　A faithful Friend is He.

And aye a loving Brother be
　Unto thy Sisters dear;
A comfort to thy Mother be,
　Her lonely heart to cheer.

How good hath thy God been to thee
　Throughout the year now gone!
His gracious hand from day to day
　Hath led thee gently on.

Then ever trust His deathless love,
　To keep thee safe from harm;
In each dark, tempted, trying hour
　Cling to His mighty arm.

Thou 'lt meet with crosses oft, my boy,
  As thou dost pass through life,
This world is but a scene of care,
  With disappointments rife.

But meet them in thy Saviour's strength,
  And thou shalt victor be,
Calmly thou 'lt journey to thy home,
  Nought e'er shall much move thee.

God bless thee, and thou shalt be blest,
  Oh ! may He keep thee ever !
In all life's duties counsel thee,
  In trials leave thee, never !

And now, on this auspicious day,
  To God I thee commend ;
Oh ! may He ever prove to thee
  Thy best, thy dearest Friend.

April 17, 1865.

WEEP NOT.

OURN not the dead—they weep never-
more,
No tear-drops are shed on that bright
shining shore ;
Their sufferings, their sorrows, their trials are o'er.
Mourn not the dead.

Mourn not the dead—they only live now,
For the amaranth crown now encircles their brow,
They gaze on the Lamb, and at His feet bow.
Mourn not the dead.

Mourn not the dead—with Jesus they rest,
Their rapture His love, and their pillow His breast,
Their companions the angels, the holy, the blest.
Mourn not the dead.

Mourn not the dead, who in Jesus are sleeping,
They now reap in joy the seed sown in weeping,
Their labours all o'er, they are safe in His keeping.
Mourn not the dead.

Mourn not the dead—they have now ceased to sin,
Eternally with God and the Lamb now shut in ;
No dark foe can enter that bright home within.
Mourn not the dead.

Mourn not the dead—round the great throne they stand,
They sing the sweet songs of the Heavenly Land,
And taste of the joys at Jesus' right hand.
     Mourn not the dead.

Mourn not the dead, who in the Lord die,
How blest are they now in the mansions on high !
Nought e'er can disturb them, no tear dims their eye.
     Mourn not the dead.

Mourn not the dead—they die nevermore,
Death's portal once past, all darkness is o'er,
Past all their conflicts, they joy evermore.
     Mourn not the dead.

May 16, 1865.

TO MARY.

TIME passes swift, dear Mary, life's but a
    fleeting dream,
    And we are carried silently adown its rapid
    stream ;
Unwittingly we move along, borne onward by the tide,
Nor e'er a moment tarry till we reach the other side.

Another year has fleeted by more swiftly than the last,
Another stage of life is run—another milestone's past ;
The wilderness still lies before, with many a dang'rous
    snare,
Replete with thorns and briars wild,—of them, my child,
    beware.

Still there are many vernal spots, and many an oasis
    sweet,
Redolent with joy—oh, mayest thou them in thy path-
    way meet ;
Beneath the palm-tree's verdant shade, when weary and
    opprest,
Oft lay thee gently down, and God shall give thee quiet
    rest.

May He with manna feed thy soul, that thou mayest
    strengthened be,
With water from the crystal rill, thine heart refresh
    may He;
That thou thy journey mayst resume, from thoughts
    unquiet free,
For walking on 'neath Love's sweet shade, how happy
    must thou be!

Oh! may the Sun of Righteousness bright on thy
    pathway shine;
In this cold, dreary winter world, a useful life be thine.
Thou enterest on another year, my Mary dear, this day;
Oh! may its hours in doing good, calm, peaceful, pass
    away.

But some days must be dark, Mary, it cannot aye be
    light;
But for the dark, we would not see the glories of the
    night.
The sun shines brightest after rain—the shade, then, do
    not fear,
For 'mid the gloom the radiant bow of mercy will ap-
    pear,

To cheer and solace thee, my child, to urge thee on
    thy way
To that bright, better, heavenly land, where reigns
    eternal day;
Bright constant shine would dazzle thee, 'twould not be
    for thy good,
Then hail a cloudlet now and then with deepest grati-
    tude.

How sweet are flow'rets after showers! how fragrant
    is the air!
So tear-drops make our graces grow, and lead the soul
    to prayer.
Then, though clouds float athwart thy sky, Jesus, thy
    Sun, is near;
The darker night, more brilliant will the gems of Heaven
    appear.

And when the desert is o'erpast, its ev'ry danger o'er,
Thou 'lt reach that land, that Home of bliss, where Love
    reigns evermore;
That golden city will unfold its pearly gates to thee,
Thou 'lt enter in, and evermore with Jesus shalt thou
    be.

June 1, 1865.

A SUMMER EVENING'S THOUGHT.

EAR Arran Isle ! once more I tread
    Thy lovely, peaceful shore,
And seated now at Invercloy,
    I think on days of yore !

When loving friends around me smiled,
    Alas ! where are they now ?
The green grass decks some lowly graves,
    Oh ! may the crown their brow.

Ne'er can those days recallèd be,
    They are for ever fled ;
Those dear loved friends, those loving hearts,
    Are number'd with the dead.

Sweet Brodick Bay, I love thee well !
    How many a tiny boat
Doth on this summer evening, calm,
    Upon thy bosom float !

Thy sky is cloudless, calm thy bay,
    Not e'en a wavelet's seen,
Whilst all around's with beauty crown'd,
    Still, solemn is the scene.

Proud Goatfell rears his lofty head
   In triumph o'er the isle ;
He seems to take a father's charge,
   And in his love to smile.

Behind Glen Rosa's solemn vale
   The sun in glory sets,
A halo bright he throws around,
   Who sees it ne'er forgets.

All Nature sleeps, deep silence reigns,
   And I am lost in thought,
My spirit soars to yonder world
   Where darkness enters not.

For as I sit, and earnest muse
   On days beyond recall,
The twilight deepens into night,
   The dews of evening fall.

Enrapt, I sit upon the shore,
   Not e'en a sound is heard—
Nought, save the murmur of the sea,
   Or praise-hymn of the bird.

I think of all the many friends
   Who used to be with me,
They scatter'd are, yea, some are gone
   Across the treacherous sea.

A sadness steals across mine heart,
   To think that nevermore
Shall we, all re-united, meet
   On this calm, tranquil shore.

Yet still I have my little ones,
  Life's lonely path to cheer;
Then deeply grateful let me be
  In having them so near.

Ah ! who can tell the future dark ?
  Revisit ne'er may we
This beauteous isle, so dear to us—
  We know not what may be.

Still let us hope that brighter days
  For us are yet in store ;
But if not, may our footsteps tread
  A brighter, happier shore.

ARRAN, *June* 15, 1865.

TO JEANIE.

EANIE, on this happy day,
Rest thee on thy homeward way,
Past's again another stage,
Of life's weary pilgrimage ;
Soon the desert will be past,
Wandering cannot always last.

Jeanie, now review the past,
All its sins on Jesus cast ;
Think what He hath done for thee ;
All His loving-kindness see ;
For the future trust His care,
He will all thy burdens bear.

Jeanie, on the wane is night,
Soon shall break the morning light,
Hour by hour 'tis drawing near,
E'en now streaks of light appear,
Heralding that perfect day
Which shall never pass away.

Jeanie, *there* can be no night,
Jesus is Heaven's glorious light,
Before that bright eternal day
Clouds shall vanish swift away ;
Cheer thee, then, it draweth nigh,
Harbingers are in the sky.

Jeanie, some days *must* be drear,
Wintry clouds will oft appear ;
As ye float adown life's stream,
Shine and shade alternate gleam ;
But if thy better Sun is nigh,
Aye serene will be thy sky.

Jeanie, happy days be thine ;
May Love on thy pathway shine.
Rest thee in a Saviour's love,
Till thou reach thy Home above—
Nought from Him can e'er thee sever,
Thou shalt reign with Him for ever.

Jeanie, in this wintry world
Storms may oft at thee be hurled ;
But if *Jesus* be thy Rock
Thou 'lt not dread the tempest's shock—
It shall pass thee harmless by,
For thou shalt on Him rely.

Jeanie, now resume thy way,
Jesus is thy Strength and Stay,
Lean on His almighty arm,
And thou shalt be free from harm ;
Should foes e'er thy peace assail,
O'er thee they shall ne'er prevail.

Jeanie, thou art loved by me,
Close friends may we ever be ;
Trusted friend of early days,
In sun and shade the same always ;
One in Jesus, are we not ?
Ransom'd by Him, precious thought !

Jeanie, may we meet in Heaven,
Where no tender ties are riven ;
Where are loved ones gone before ;
Where the tear falls nevermore !
Where with Jesus we shall be !
Rest with Him eternally !

November 8, 1865.

TO A ROSEBUD.

ENTLE sweet flow'ret, the child of a day,
How passing's thy beauty! it swift fadeth
away;
Dost thou, fair rosebud, bloom but to
decay?
Echo—bloom but to decay!

I fain would thee keep, oh! wilt thou not stay,
To cheer my sad heart in the cold wintry day?
But thou canst not, ah! no, thou 'rt swift passing away.
Echo—swift passing away!

Meet emblem of man, whose frail house of clay,
Like all things of earth, dures but a short day,
To dust it returns, and so passeth away.
Echo—so passeth away!

Farewell, then, bright rosebud, if thus it must be,
How solemn the lesson which thou teachest me!
In thy beauty God's love, power, and goodness I see
Echo—and goodness I see!

December 7, 1865.

NEW YEAR'S HYMN.

ONLY WAITING.

THE Old Year is gone, and a New Year is
    dawning,
    How surely Time passes, on swift, silent
    wing!
How full of instruction! how solemn the warning,
  Which circling years must to the thoughtful mind
    bring!

The night of earth waneth, its shining and shading,
  Its fears and its doubtings, shall all pass away;
Its smiles and its tears, its blooming and fading,
  Its joys and its sorrows, all, all must decay.

Yes! night is far spent, Heaven's day is now breaking,
  The dawn is disclosing a bright, restful shore,
A short, fitful dream, then a glorious awaking,
  To feel all the ills of this weary life o'er.

In the Year now gone by, from this valley of weeping
  How many a loved one has swift past away!
But the jewel is safe in the Saviour's own keeping,
  'Tis the casket alone that can e'er know decay.

Sweet buds and gay flow'rets, the Reaper, not scorning,
Transplanted to bloom in God's garden above;
He needed them there—that Home now adorning,
They shine evermore in the light of His love.

Then cheer thee, O mourner! thy loved ones in glory
With God and the Lamb rejoice evermore,
'Mid the fair bowers of Eden, retracing life's story,
Their tears are all wept, and their sorrows all o'er.

And ere this New Year close, thou, too, mayst be sleep-
ing,
O'er thy lone, lowly bed sweet flow'rets may bloom;
But may Arms Everlasting be thee safely keeping,
In the spirit-land bright, beyond the dark tomb.

The Bridegroom approaches! His footsteps are nearing!
E'en *now* is His voice loud proclaiming, "I come!"
With joy shall His ransomed all hail His appearing,
Their lamps burning brightly, He'll welcome them
home.

But art thou preparèd for that solemn meeting?
For soon shall the trumpet sound, Time be no more:
Shall the "Well done" of Jesus be thy welcome greet-
ing,
When called to appear God's tribunal before?

If "Behold, I come quickly!" in thine ears should be
sounded,
Oh! canst thou respond, "E'en so, Lord Jesus,
come"?
Thy full tide of joy then shall roll on unbounded,
His Love shall thy Heaven be, His bosom thy Home.

But if not, take heed, and list to the warning,
  'Tis the sweet voice of Jesus which now calls to thee,
In tenderest accents, on this New Year's morning,
  " Awake ! thou that sleepest, and come unto Me.

" *My* peace shall be thine, flowing on as a river,
  Till lost in the depths of the Ocean above ;
Not thy sins, not thy follies, can thee from Me sever,
  As a seal on Mine heart I have set thee in love."

To the poor trembling sinner, those words, oh, how
    cheering !
  To have Jesus as Saviour, as Brother, as Friend!
To call God " Our Father," what name so endearing !
  The Spirit, as Guide, till the day of grace end.

Oh ! come, then, lone wand'rer, list the voice of Love
    calling,
Reject not salvation so full and so free ;
  To Calvary flee, before the Cross falling,
Behold what the Saviour has done, and for thee.

" Remember me, Lord," be thy soul's earnest pleading ;
  How gracious the answer! " Thy wanderings are
    o'er ;
E'en now I'm in glory for thee interceding,
  In My changeless love rest thee, and be glad ever-
    more."

In this dark vale of Baca there's nought that abideth,
  Black clouds float athwart e'en the brightest of skies;
But if thy soul, pilgrim, in Jesus confideth,
  Thy faith is unclouded, thy hope never dies.

'Tis anchor'd on Jesus, the True, the Unchanging,
  Ah! then, how secure 'midst the deadliest strife!
From pleasure to pleasure thou ne'er think'st of rang-
    ing,
  For *Jesus* is with thee, the Life of thy life.

Though thy sky be as midnight, thy Sun ever shineth,
  No clouds can enshroud Him from thine eagle eye;
Thou piercest the darkness, thy day ne'er declineth,
  No night canst thou know—aye serene is thy sky.

In the hot, fiery furnace, the gold God refineth,
  Till He sees mirror'd forth His own image bright,
So the Christian, afflicted, nor faints, nor repineth—
  He knows 'tis Love's hand that's uplifted to smite.

The hand of a *Father*, so gentle, so loving,
  Who draws the lone, chastened one close to His
    breast,
Then kiss the rod meekly, thy trust in Him proving,
  Lay thine head on His bosom, *there* only is rest.

For the children of God there's a rest that remaineth
  When the tears and the fears of this desert are o'er,
A home for the weary, where peace ever reigneth,
  Where the Lamb is its glory, its light evermore!

But for that perfect rest is thy soul now preparing?
  Hast thou fled to the Saviour for pardon and peace?
Is He to thee precious, beyond all comparing?
  Then thou 'lt joy in believing, all terrors shall cease.

But if this vain world thine all thou 'rt esteeming,
　If its joys and its pleasures oft lead thee astray,
Beware, oh ! beware, lest Time, not redeeming,
　Thy fond, cherish'd treasures swift vanish away !'

In this wilderness lone oft thine heart may be failing,
　Way-worn and weary, home is oft lost to view,
By dangers surrounded, foes by night thee assailing,
　Yet the cloud and fire-pillar shall lead thee safe
　　through.

Resume, then, thy journey, though " faint, yet pur-
　　suing,"
　Nor linger amid the gay pleasures of Time,
And Jesus, thine heart with fresh courage renewing,
　Shall safe thee conduct to a happier clime.

Through all this new year rest on thee God's bless-
　　ing,
　May He keep thee, and guide thee, with His own
　　gentle hand,
To cheer thee when sad, as homeward thou 'rt press-
　　ing,
　Thee a vista-glimpse give of the bright Holy Land.

Then forward, O pilgrim ! though thy path may seem
　　dreary,
　Thy Saviour hath trodden its rough footsteps before,
His arm is around thee to uphold thee when weary,
　His strength shall be thine till thy journey is o'er.

Still upward! still onward! thy daily cross bearing,
The way may be toilsome, but it cannot be long,
Then in thy bright mansion, the crown of life wearing,
Thou 'lt chant with the ransomed, the Old, the New
Song!

January 1, 1866.

NEW-YEAR'S HYMN FOR CHILDREN.

JESUS! Thou who art "*the Way*,"
Guide Thy little lamb each day,
Keep, oh! keep me, lest I stray,
    All through this New Year.

Jesus! Thou who art "*the Truth*,"
Be the Teacher of my youth,
Lead me in the paths of truth,
    All through this New Year.

Jesus! Thou who art "*the Life*,"
When with foes my path is rife,
Aid and shield me in the strife,
    All through this New Year.

Jesus! Thou who art "*the Vine*,"
Clasp my feeble hand in Thine,
Sweetly whisper, "Thou art Mine,"
    All through this New Year.

Jesus! Thou who art "*the Light*,"
Shine and cheer me in the night,
Make each dark day calm and bright,
    All through this New Year.

Jesus! Thou who art "*The Rest*,"
When I'm weary and opprest,
Fold me to Thy gentle breast,
    All through this New Year!

January 1, 1866.

TO LIZZIE.

WIFTLY has another year
Fleeted by, my Lizzie dear ;
Time is gliding fast away,
Dawned's again thy natal day,
Days and years are hasting on—
Soon will life's short reign be done.

Twenty summers hast thou seen,
Led and cared for hast thou been ;
God has been thy Father, Friend,
And He'll be so till life end ;
If thou on His love rely,
He will all thy wants supply.

Choose, oh ! choose the Better Part !
Give to Jesus thy young heart ;
Remember Him in early youth,
He'll thee lead in paths of truth.
Oh ! to Him commit thy way,
He will guide thee day by day.

Should thy path be ever drear,
Jesus, thy best Friend, is near ;
He will mark thine ev'ry sigh,
Wipe each tear-drop from thine eye,
Whisper words of healing balm,
Turn each storm into a calm.

Fear not then the tempest's shock,
Jesus is thy sheltering Rock;
Winds may roar, and waves may beat,
Thou hast aye a safe retreat;
Danger ne'er can thee betide,
If thou nestle in His side.

Storms shall pass thee harmless by,
If thou walk beneath His eye;
Calm thou 'lt be, though billows rage,
Jesus will their wrath assuage;
Though clouds gather, thou shalt smile,
Jesus shall their gloom beguile.

This is but a vale of gloom,
Each dark scene do thou illume,
To all around a sunbeam be,
So shall life pass cheerily;
All shall hail thy presence bright,
Where was darkness shall be light.

There's a vacant chair this year
At our board, my Lizzie dear;
Oh! how solemn is the thought,
That he is gone, that he is not;
He who was so fond of thee,
Nevermore on earth we 'll see.

Hushed is that loving, happy voice,
Which bade thy youthful heart rejoice;
But, oh! is he not happier far
Shining bright as brightest star?
On his day shall fall no night,
Where he now is all is light.

There! may we in God's time meet,
In Jesus glorified, complete.
There! He is our All in All;
There! no tear-drop e'er can fall;
There! beyond the darksome tomb,
There all's peace, and joy, and bloom!

January 13, 1866.

AN IMPROMPTU.

INE own sweet child, my Lizzie's gone,
She now rests before the throne;
Short the race she had to run,
Now the happy goal is won;
She's not lost, but gone before;
Now she liveth evermore.

Away from this dark scene of strife,
Radiant with immortal life,
She the crown of glory wears,
She the palm of triumph bears,
With the holy ransomed throng
Chants the sweet, eternal song.

She with Jesus walks in white
In that land of love and light,
Him follows wheresoe'er He leads,
By waters still or verdant meads,
Culling never-fading flowers
From its amaranthine bowers.

She nor sin nor sorrow knows,
Her tide of joy for ever flows;
Let us then not selfish be,
But picture her felicity,
And prepare her steps to follow—
Spend with her Heaven's bright to-morrow.

March 2, 1866.

TO TOM.

INE own dear boy, another year
Of thy life's fleeting, short career
Hath sped on noiseless wing away,
And sad must be thy thoughts this day,
For she to whom thine heart was wed
Is number'd with the silent dead.

But list her loving angel voice,
Bidding thee with her rejoice,
That *now* her sufferings all are o'er,
That *now* she sorrows nevermore,
That our deep loss is her great gain,
For *now* she's free from sin and pain.

And though each day we miss her more,
She is not lost, but gone before;
In the bright mansions of the blest,
She doth on Jesus' bosom rest;
For ever done with care and strife,
She bloometh in immortal life.

Oh! could we but see her now!
The crown encircling that fair brow,
The palm of triumph in her hand,
Singing the songs of that bright land,
Clad in a robe of dazzling whiteness,
Scarce could one gaze on its brightness.

Then let us all prepare to follow,
And pass with her a bright to-morrow ;
May we all meet before the throne,
Hear Jesus claim us as His own ;
Not one awanting, may we spend
A holy Sabbath, without end.

Choose *now*, my boy, the Better Part ;
Give *now* to God thy youthful heart,
Him love and serve in manhood's prime,
The warning list, " Redeem the time."
All things are fleeting here below,
This world is but a scene of woe.

Be thine the Christian's useful life,
Resist temptations, envy, strife ;
The cause of God and truth promote—
Thy talents all to Him devote ;
So shall thy days glide calm away,
For He will be thy Strength, thy Stay.

How solemn are the changes here!
Two empty chairs in one short year.
Two from our home have past away—
How loving and how loved were they !
Their weary wanderings all are o'er,
And now they rest for evermore.

And as our circle narrows here,
Oh ! may it widen in that sphere,
Where no tender ties are riven,
For, ah ! there is no death in Heaven ;
There all partings are unknown,
There we shall in heart be one.

See Love inscribed on each dark cloud;
E'en though it wear the blackest shroud,
Behind it is a Father's smile.
This will the dreary gloom beguile ,
He loves thee, else He would not smite,
He's nearest thee in darkest night.

Then brave, dear boy, tread life's rough way,
Soon will it end in brightest day,
List to the still small voice of Love—
" I'll lead thee till thou rest above;
If thou wilt only trust in Me,
Ere long thou shalt *My* glory see."

And now to God I thee commend,
Thee may He keep till life shall end !
Thy mother's prayers are thine this day,
Her love, my boy, shall ne'er decay.
O happy, happy may'st thou be,
Now, and to all Eternity !

April 17, 1866.

TO MARY.

 N this auspicious, happy day,
Too sad I fear will be my lay,
For what I would I cannot say,
   My Mary.

Since last I wrote thee on this day,
Our dear wee pet has past away
From the frail tenement of clay,
   My Mary.

Our loved one doth in Jesus sleep,
And He doth sweet watch o'er her keep,
Then dry the tear-drop from thy cheek,
   My Mary.

A changeful year has been the last,
Wave upon wave has o'er thee past,
Death has his dark shade o'er thee cast,
   My Mary.

And though ofttimes thou lonely art,
May Jesus cheer thine aching heart,
His heavenly, healing balm impart,
   My Mary.

Could we but see her now on high,
With beaming face and sparkling eye,
We would not shed a tear nor sigh,
                    My Mary.

For she is happier far than we ;
From sin, from sorrow she is free ;
How holy and how blest is she !
                    My Mary.

And though we miss her very sore,
Yea, daily mourn her more and more,
She treads a brighter, happier shore,
                    My Mary.

And should dark clouds e'er gloom thy sky,
Oh ! fear not, Jesus will be nigh,
To wipe the tear-drop from thine eye,
                    My Mary.

He 'll cheer thee in the darkest night,
Put gloom and sadness all to flight,
Then walk with Him, for He is light,
                    My Mary.

The furnace-fires are to refine,
When in them cast do not repine,
They 're but a proof of love divine,
                    My Mary.

If thou the crown of life would wear,
Meek, Christ-like, thou the Cross must bear
Without a fear, without a care,
                    My Mary.

Oh ! seest thou that happy band,
Who round the throne of glory stand ?
All they have kiss'd God's chastening hand,
My Mary.

A loving daughter aye thou art,
Thou cheerest oft thy mother's heart,
Now bleeding 'neath affliction's smart,
My Mary.

Many a happy year be thine,
God bless thee with His love divine,
And cause on thee His face to shine,
My Mary.

No ; I can never, never be,
What "Little Ethie" was to thee,
So precious was her sympathy,
My Mary.

Oh ! list her angel-voice this day,
"The rising tear, dear Sissie, stay,
And onward, homeward, urge thy way,
My Mary.

"What I now am, thou soon shalt be ;
Nought e'er shall sever thee and me,
All through a bright eternity,
My Mary."

Earth's fairest flowers must fade and die,
Heaven's flow'rets bloom beyond the sky ;
There look with Faith's all-hopeful eye,
My Mary.

And see our cherish'd flow'ret there,
In beauty blooming, oh how fair !
'Neath cloudless skies, and balmy air,
     My Mary.

And when life's toilsome journey 's o'er,
Oh ! may we meet on yon bright shore,
Where are our loved ones gone before,
     My Mary.

O may we meet them in that home,
Where no chill blast can o'er us come,
And from which we no more shall roam !
     My Mary.

There we 'll meet, no more to sever !
There we 'll part no more for ever !
There we 'll sin, we 'll sorrow, never !
     My Mary.

June 1, 1866.

A SUNSET.

HE, the true, the noble-hearted,
From this scene has now departed
And entered on his rest ;
Oh ! our great loss is his true gain,
For he hath done with sin and pain—
Is with the faithful blest.

Long was the race he had to run,
Reach'd was the goal at set of sun,
A sunset, peaceful, calm.
Peace, love, and joy now thrill his breast,
In Jesus' love he now doth rest—
He bears the triumph palm.

Now ended is his long campaign,
For now he doth with Jesus reign,
All, all is glory now.
The amaranthine crown of life,
Given to each victor in the strife,
Encircles now his brow.

As sad child on a mother's breast,
Lull'd by her gentle voice to rest,
Does all its wailings cease,
So did he calmly fall asleep ;
He saw not us who sad did weep
Around his couch of peace.

The face of man he never feared,
Aye to the cause of truth adhered,
   A champion bold was he.
The widow's plea he aye sustained,
The orphan's rights he aye maintained—
   Ne'er daunted could he be.

He closed his eyes on earthly things,
He heard the flap of angel-wings,
   Beckoning him away
To that fair land where all is bright;
Where *Jesus* is, there is no night,
   But perfect, cloudless day.

The oldest and the youngest gone
Together now before the throne,
   Rejoicing with the blest.
How he would welcome " Little Tot,"
The wee pet whom he ne'er forgot,
   To Jesus' peaceful breast.

For ten weeks only were they parted,
Us leaving well-nigh broken-hearted,
   Now side by side they sleep.
Nought e'er shall mar their deep repose,
The storms of earth and all its woes
   No more shall o'er them sweep.

They sleep in Jesus, blessèd sleep,
He o'er their dust doth vigil keep
   In yonder hallowed spot.
Bright angels guard their lowly bed,
Then why weep o'er the holy dead ?
   Their God forgets them not.

And when is heard in yonder cloud,
The trump of God proclaiming loud
   That time shall no more be,
Oh ! may we all arise, awake,
When that bright MORN of morns shall break,
   Where there is no more sea.

June 23, 1866.

WAITING.

HOW long, O Lord, how long?
Is oft the afflicted's cry.
Not long, my child, not long,
Is Jesus' sweet reply.

How long, O Lord, how long,
Ere past's this desert drear?
Not long, my child, not long,
The heavenly land is near.

How long, O Lord, how long,
Ere my short race be run?
Not long, my child, not long,
Till yon bright goal be won.

How long, O lord, how long,
Ere my barque reach the port?
Not long, my child, not long,
Though now of storms the sport.

How long, O Lord, how long,
Ere my campaign be o'er?
Not long, my child, not long,
Then glory evermore.

How long, O Lord, how long,
  Will last this weary strife?
Not long, my child, not long,
  Then thine a crown of life.

How long, O Lord, how long,
  Ere I have done with sin?
Not long, my child, not long,
  Till holiness thou win.

How long, O Lord, how long,
  Shall I my loved one weep?
Not long, my child, not long—
  Thyself shalt fall asleep.

How long, O Lord, how long,
  Ere pain and toil be o'er?
Not long, my child, not long—
  All's rest on this calm shore.

How long, O Lord, how long,
  Ere I the last tear shed?
Not long, my child, not long,
  Till ev'ry trace be fled.

How long, O Lord, how long,
  Ere all heart-burnings cease?
Not long, my child, not long,
  Till thou shalt share my peace.

How long, O Lord, how long,
  Shall I my crosses bear?
Not long, my child, not long,
  Till thou the bright crown wear.

How long, O Lord, how long,
  Ere I do see Thy face?
Not long, my child, not long,
  Till thou rest in mine embrace.

How long, O Lord, how long,
  Ere I do reach my home?
Not long, my child, not long,
  Until Love's Angel come.

How long, O Lord, how long,
  Ere I in glory be?
Not long, my child, not long,
  Until I welcome thee.

How long, O Lord, how long,
  Not then shall be the cry!
Not long, my child, not long,
  Shall not be the reply!

For aye, O Lord, for aye,
  Shall then my sweet song be!
For aye, my child, for aye,
  Thou shalt My glory see!

For aye, O Lord, for aye,
  Shall I be holy, blest!
For aye, my child, for aye,
  Thou shalt in My love rest!

July 1, 1866.

IN MEMORIAM.

AH! can it be that thou art gone, gone from
my fond embrace!
That nevermore on earth I'll see thy bright,
thy sunny face!
Oh! I cannot think it is so, I think thou still art here—
That soon thou wilt return to me, and then I stay the
tear.

Ah! this is but a sunny gleam, ere falls the thunder
shower;
I look around in vain, alas! gone is my treasured
flower;
Then o'er me steals the pensive thought, thou'lt ne'er
come back to me,
But at the most, a few short years, and I shall go to
thee.

Husht is thy merry, ringing voice, ne'er shall I hear it
more;
Still is thy lightsome footfall, oh! I do miss it sore;
Thou treadest now the golden streets, amid the
ransom'd throng,
Thy voice, in sweet seraphic strains, swells the unending
song.

Thou bloomest in a sunnier clime, whose skies are aye
    serene ;
The Tree of Life o'ershadows thee, whose leaf is ever
    green.
Beneath His branches thou dost rest beside Life's crystal
    river,
Clad in immortal loveliness, thy bloom shall fade, ah !
    never.

Hand joined in hand, we daily met before the throne of
    grace,
To tell our Father all our sins, and seek His gracious face ;
O ! may we meet in lowly praise before the throne of
    glory,
And through Heaven's blissful, endless days, recount
    salvation's story.

Oh ! not long parted shall we be, time hastens on
    apace—
E'en now the goal may be in view, soon run may be my
    race ;
Full many a chink is being made in this frail house of
    clay,
Ere long ' twill totter and fall down, my spirit flee away.

Thou 'lt hail me at the pearly gates, sweet shall our
    meeting be,
Thou 'lt lead me to the Saviour's feet, that He may
    welcome me ;
The bitter pang of parting then, nor felt, nor feared is
    more,
For ah ! the mournful word, " farewell," is known not
    on that shore !

An early crown is thine, my child, soon meet for
    Heaven wert thou,
Thy robes washed white in Jesus' blood, how radiant
    are they now !
Could I but realise thy bliss, I'd not so selfish be ;
I'd meekly say, " God's will be done, in love He
    chastens me."

He has me cast into the fires, but oh ! I'll not repine,
I'll kiss the rod my Father holds, 'tis needed discipline.
In this lone heart a blank's been made, which nought on
    earth can fill,
E'en so it seemèd good to God—then, O my soul, be still.

I would not call thee back to earth, thou only livest *now*,
All glorious is thy glistening robe and crown-encircled
    brow !
Thy day of death thy birth-day was, to endless life and
    joy,
For in our Father's house above there's bliss without
    alloy.

God's high behests thou dost fulfil, thou mayest watch
    o'er me,
But for this veil of mortal flesh, thine angel face I'd see;
I cannot picture all thy bliss, 'tis deep—*too* deep for me,
But with my soul's eye I can view thy full felicity.

The beauty of eternal youth shall never fade away,
The grace of perfect sinlessness shall never know
    decay ;
I know that thou art happier far than when thou wert
    with me—
Thou baskest in the Sun of Love, dost all His glory see.

I could not think that thou wert gone, as I clasp'd thee
    to my breast,
I little thought thy happy soul had entered into rest;
Thou didst so gently close thine eyes, go from my fond
    embrace,
To open them in Jesus' arms, and see Him face to face.

Methinks it would have been too much for thy gentle,
    loving heart,
To bid us all a long farewell, and from us all to part;
So God in mercy spared thee this—thou sweetly fell
    asleep—
For sure it would have grieved thee sore to see thy
    loved ones weep.

Thy sudden death to thee, my child, would sudden
    glory be—
The visions that would meet thy gaze would glorious be
    to thee;
The voice of Jesus, oh, how sweet! would bid thee
    welcome home,
And sainted ones would echo loud, " Oh! come, sweet
    sister, come."

Death's dreary vale no terrors had, all seemed so peace-
    ful, bright;
No valley-gloom encompass'd thee, for *Jesus* was its
    light—
No King of Terrors called thee hence, 'twas Jesus'
    voice of love
That summoned thee from earth away, to thy bright
    home above.

Thy little hand clasp'd fast in mine, this was thy last request,
" My mammie, I am vext for you—do go and take a
rest."
These words of fond endearment to me were scarcely
spoken,
Ere loosened was the silver cord, and the golden bowl
was broken.

The heavenly look I'll ne'er forget, that settled on thy
brow,
As thou didst calmly fall asleep—methinks I see it now ;
It seemed as if the glories of thy mansion in the sky
Had burst upon thy raptured sight in all their ma-
jesty.

The Reaper came and culled my flower, so graceful and
so fair,
That in God's garden it might bloom, safe tended by
His care.
And now my Lily's gathered to the Paradise above,
God needed her, to grace and gem the Eden of His
love.

Thou wert a flow'ret far too fair, my precious, angel
child,
To brave the storms of this cold world or face its tempests wild,
So Jesus took thee to His Home, to blossom 'neath His
eye,
That peaceful Home where no chill blight can e'er to
thee come nigh.

And God will give thee back to me, more beautiful,
    more fair,
Than when He took thee from mine arms, to grow in
    beauty there;
He will not linger overlong, only one little hour,
Then I shall in mine embrace fold my fondly-treasured
    flower.

Oh, the rapture of that moment! its blissfulness, how
    sweet!
When you and I in that bright home for evermore shall
    meet;
E'en now this thought is cheering, it soothes this bleed-
    ing heart,
To know that when we meet again, we meet no more
    to part.

Till then I'll wait my Father's time, for it is alway best,
Though sad and weary oft I be, come *will* the hour of
    rest;
It may be in that solemn hour, when I shall fall asleep,
My loved one o'er her mother's couch a silent watch
    may keep.

From thee, my beauteous flow'ret, hard, hard it was to
    part,
So close wert thou entwined around the tendrils of my
    heart—
'Twas almost death to sever us, to snap Love's golden
    chain,
That linked thy loving heart to mine, alas! 'tis snapt in
    twain.

How close the tie that bound our souls, none save our
    God can know,
No wonder then that from this heart the tears unceasing
    flow ;
Its wounds are ever bleeding sore, its anguish, who can
    tell ?
He only who hath dealt the blow, who doeth all things
    well.

What bliss, what joy ineffable, shall thrill our raptured
    heart,
To feel that from our Saviour-God nought ever shall
    us part !
That we shall bloom eternally in that bright, Better
    Land,
And taste the joys and pleasures which·are at His right
    hand.

O ! may we there together bloom, and all our gathered
    flowers
In grace and holy beauty grow 'mid Eden's vernal
    bowers ;
Upon a harp of gold we'll sing the praises of the Lamb,
And join with saints and angels in the deep, unending
    Psalm.

All there is perfect *holiness*, sin cannot enter Heaven !
All there is perfect *happiness*, no loving hearts are riven !
All there is perfect *peacefulness*, waves break not on that
    shore!
All there is perfect *restfulness*, toil's ended evermore !

All there is perfect *joyfulness*, unsullied by a tear!

All there is perfect *trustfulness*, without a shade of fear!

All there is perfect *knowledge*, for Faith is changed to Sight!

All there is perfect, endless *day*, without the fear of night!

July 15, 1866.

Printed by Neill and Company, Edinburgh.